ARTIE

AND THE GRIME WAVE

ARTIE
AND THE GRIME WAVE

written and illustrated by

Richard Roxburgh

ALLEN&UNWIN
SYDNEY · MELBOURNE · AUCKLAND · LONDON

First published by Allen & Unwin in 2016

Allen & Unwin
83 Alexander Street
Crows Nest NSW 2065
Australia
Phone: (61 2) 8425 0100
Email: info@allenandunwin.com
Web: www.allenandunwin.com

A Cataloguing-in-Publication entry is available from the National
Library of Australia
www.trove.nla.gov.au

ISBN 978 1 76029 214 0

Cover and text design by Liz Seymour
Set in 13.5 pt Garamond Classico by Liz Seymour
Printed and bound in Australia by Griffin Press
Inside back cover photo by Eva Rinaldi

10 9 8 7 6 5 4 3 2 1

MIX
Paper from
responsible sources
FSC® C009448

The paper in this book is FSC® certified.
FSC® promotes environmentally responsible,
socially beneficial and economically viable
management of the world's forests.

Contents

Chapter 1 PAPERBARK SHOES 1

Chapter 2 THE CAVE-OF-POSSIBLY-STOLEN-STUFF 12

Chapter 3 WOLF!!! 17

Chapter 4 THE CAVE-OF-ALMOST-CERTAINLY-STOLEN-STUFF 22

Chapter 5 POWDER LOLLIES 29

Chapter 6 PROOF 37

Chapter 7 GRAYSTAINS 43

Chapter 8 MARY 51

Chapter 9 SIDECAR 56

Chapter 10 NEW FRIENDS 63

Chapter 11 BUNGEE-WEDGIE 71

Chapter 12 THE RIVER 80

Chapter 13 PURPLE SOUP 84

Chapter 14 STAR JUMPS 90

Chapter 15 THE FARTEX 120Y 97

Chapter 16 ONION PUFFS 106

Chapter 17 DARK 112

Chapter 18 GRIME HOUSE 118

Chapter 19 COCKERDOODLE CUTLET 127

Chapter 20 THE STATUE 135

Chapter 21 SIZE 14 CHEF'S CLEAVER 143

Chapter 22 GARETH 153

Chapter 23 PRIME CUTS 156

Chapter 24 INTO THE UNKNOWN 165

Chapter 25 GOLF 174

Chapter 26 A BIT OF A MISSION 179

Chapter 27 THE LEANING TOWER OF BUMSHOES 182

Chapter 28 RENOVATIONS 191

Chapter 29 UKRAINIAN OLYMPIC DISCUS
CHAMPION, 1996 197

Chapter 30 FLU-SNOT 202

Chapter 31 THE FLYING TRAPEZE 206

Chapter 32 AND THEN WHAT HAPPENED? 216

But of course,
to
Silvia, Raphael and Miro

Chapter 1

Paperbark Shoes

Artie's shoes dangled over the electrical wires, bobbing lightly in the breeze, as if an invisible dancer was doing a weird little jig. All the boys gazed up at them, and Artie squashed his lips into a tight little line to keep from crying. He knew there was no stick long enough to poke them down, and anyway, everybody knows you don't go prodding around near power lines.

Nate and his friend Wart were falling about with laughter. Nate Grime had frizzy hair and tiny eyes like two bunny droppings on a bowl of porridge. Nate's dad, Mr Grime, was the mayor of the town, a fact that Nate never failed to mention.

Nate seemed to spend most of his life devising ever-more-imaginative ways of torturing Artie Small.

So far this had included:

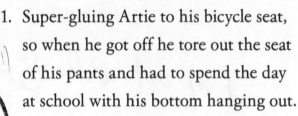

1. Super-gluing Artie to his bicycle seat, so when he got off he tore out the seat of his pants and had to spend the day at school with his bottom hanging out.

2. Stealing his swimmers on carnival day so that he had to swim in his undies.

3. Taking his lunch box while he was in science class and cramming his sandwiches with flies and what may have been boogers (he didn't taste them to find out).

4. Loading his sports shorts with stinking brown mud, so that all through P.E. it looked as if he'd had a terrible accident.

And now this: ambushing Artie on the way home from school, tearing his shoes off and flinging them up over the power lines.

'HAHAHAHA. How yer gonna get 'em down, eh, Farty Artie?' Nate squawked.

'Don't know ...' Artie mumbled, gazing at the ground.

Nate's best mate, Wart, was oversized in all ways apart from his forehead, which looked like it belonged to someone much smaller. This gave him the vague appearance of a silverback gorilla on a bicycle. Wart ate onions like other kids eat apples, and through a mouthful of onion mush, he yelled, 'HAHAHA. Check out the holes ... HAHAHA. Holes in his socks!'

It was true. Artie stared at those holes, his toes and heels exposed on both feet. Artie's friend, Bumshoe, nudged him.

'C'mon,' he whispered without moving his mouth. 'Ready?'

Artie gave a little nod.

Bumshoe pointed at thin air and screamed:

'RABBITS!!!'

Nate and Wart, momentarily disarmed, looked around open-mouthed, and in this nanosecond Artie and Bumshoe made their escape. Bumshoe *always* played the rabbit trick on

the gang and, incredibly, they *always* fell for the same thing. It seemed that if you yelled 'Rabbits' loud enough, it was possible to send not-particularly-bright people into a temporary state of mental confusion, and in that brief moment, escapes could be enacted.

Furious and humiliated at yet again having fallen foul of the rabbit trick, Nate leapt on his bike and gave chase, Wart whizzing along behind him. Artie and Bumshoe, terrified for their lives, tore off down the hill on their bikes as fast as their legs would pedal (two chubby and pink, and two bony, white and shoe-less).

Fortunately, there is nothing like blind terror to get smallish legs moving at supersonic speed. Soon Artie and Bumshoe had outpaced their foes and then lost them entirely. At last they could stop and regain their breath.

Artie Small was twelve but, true to his name, quite small. He lived with his mum and sister. His dad had died some years before, and ever since then his mum, Maggie, had spent every day in her dressing-gown, lying on her bed or the sofa, and never leaving the house. Shopping for groceries, cooking meals and cleaning were all left to Artie and his sister, Lola, who was nearly sixteen. Lola spent almost every waking moment messaging on her phone and when she wasn't, she was *spectacularly,* *mind-blowingly,* *gobsmackingly* cranky.

Artie's only real friend was Bumshoe, whose actual name was Alex Baumschule, but it always come out sounding like Bumshoe, so at some point Bumshoe had stopped correcting everyone. Now the whole world, even teachers, called Bumshoe Bumshoe. Bumshoe *(I'm sorry for putting so many Bumshoes together like that, dear reader, and I'll try and make sure it doesn't happen again)* lived with his dad and about five million brothers and sisters in a grungy little house in the swampy part of town. His house reminded Artie of the nursery rhyme about the old lady who lived in a shoe, only at Bumshoe's house there was no lady, because Bumshoe's mum had run off with a skiing instructor from Finland.

Artie and Bumshoe were like bookends: Bumshoe only had a dad and Artie only had a mum, and neither boy saw very much of his parent in any case …

Bumshoe had freckles and a fringe and was as chubby as Artie was scrawny. His diet consisted mostly of junk food, especially Chococaramel-Cococreambombs. They were his lolly of choice, and his pockets were always plugged full of them.

The boys rode through the outskirts of the town, past the famous statue of Mayor Grime that greeted any traffic

coming inwards. It had been
purchased by Mrs Grime and
given as a 'gift to the town'.
It was a bizarre and
humungous representation
of Mayor Grime as the Roman
god Jupiter, complete with
lightning bolt and shield,
and it never failed to set
the boys laughing out
loud as they passed it.

Dripping with
sweat and radish-
red, Bumshoe at
last stopped on a
dirt track and shook
a bag of Chococaramel- Cococreambombs at his friend. By now
they'd cycled all the way up Nail Can Hill. Things normally
felt better to Artie up there, surrounded by trees and sky. But
today was different …

'My mum's going to face-plant!' Artie exclaimed. 'I've only
got the one pair of shoes, and now they're up a telephone pole.'

Bumshoe, who always had ideas about *everything*, gazed about for a moment, considering his friend's plight and trying to chew the tennis ball–sized lump of squished-up lolly-goo in his mouth.

'Ooo,' he exclaimed. 'I know! We coo' ma' some shoesh ou' o' paperbaaaaa'.

Because Bumshoe's cheeks were always full of mashed-up lollies, Artie had become the world's leading expert at translating his mashed-up words.

'Make shoes out of *paperbark*?' Artie repeated.

Bumshoe tried to swallow the great lump in his cheek. 'I've read about it. The ancient tribes used to do it! You'll build yourself some top-notch shoes from paperbark, don't you worry! And ...' at this point he wriggled his eyebrows, 'I know where all the paperbark trees are ...'

'It's a mental idea,' said Artie.

'You might start a new fashion!' said Bumshoe, fossicking around for another lolly. 'What could possibly go wrong?'

It *was* a mental idea, Artie remained convinced. His mum was still going to face-plant – in fact she'd face-plant even harder when he strolled into the house wearing paperbark shoes!

But Bumshoe was his friend. And sometimes you just have to go along with your friends, even when they have mental ideas.

Soon the boys had abandoned their bikes by the side of the dirt track and were battling their way through thick scrub.

'Funny. I could've sworn those paperbark trees were just … up … here,' puffed Bumshoe. Artie's feet, clad in what were now barely recognisable as socks, were scratched and sore from prickles and sticks.

'Ouch. Ouch. Ow,' he complained. 'Let's go home! I can get some shoes at the charity shop. The ladies always give me freebies in there!'

In fact, Artie hated going into the charity shop and having to ask for things, even though the ladies were always lovely and made a big fuss over him, giving him tea and biscuits and asking if everything was alright at home. It was really embarrassing, and he'd do anything to avoid it. Anything, that is, apart from wearing paperbark shoes.

'Just … at the top … of this … hill, I reckon,' grunted his friend.

In that instant Bumshoe froze, causing Artie's face to run smack-bang into his hefty buttocks and nearly sending both of them sprawling.

'Shhhhhhhhhhhhhhhhh!!' hissed Bumshoe.

Artie peered over his friend's shoulder.

'What do you reckon it is?' whispered Bumshoe urgently, pointing down the hill.

Artie shook his head, his heart thumping in his chest …

Chapter 2

The Cave-of-Possibly-Stolen-Stuff

A few metres below them was a grassy clearing that backed onto a steep rock wall. In the middle of the wall was a cave entrance. A rough dirt track led into the cleared area, in which a van and motorbike were parked. Bumshoe turned to Artie, his eyes like ping-pong balls.

'Will we take a look?' he whispered intently.

'S'pose so …' nodded Artie meekly. The fact of the matter was that Artie hated adventures, and tried to avoid them at all cost. He remembered his dad saying 'Most of the best discoveries in life happen when you step into the unknown' – and he should have known, he was a tightrope walker and trapeze artist in the circus! As scary and dangerous as his work was, Artie's dad had simply become sick one day and died soon after. Ever since, Artie had decided that life was tricky enough without adding unnecessary scary bits.

He was secretly hoping his friend might come to the same realisation when Bumshoe began creeping down through the bushes on all fours like an immense, sweaty wombat. Artie reluctantly followed behind, becoming aware of an increasingly unpleasant stench. 'Whoooooa!' Bumshoe suddenly stopped once more, and Artie nearly ran into him yet again. His friend teetered on the edge of a deep, stinking hole with a swarm of flies buzzing around it. They had clearly stumbled onto, and nearly into, a pit that had been dug as a toilet. Bumshoe turned to Artie, clamped his fingers over his nose and screwed up his face to signify *STENCH!* Delicately skirting around the awful hole, they picked their way to the edge of the clearing. The place seemed deserted.

'C'mon,' whispered Bumshoe as he broke out and galloped towards the cave. As he ran he doubled over, as if that would somehow make him less visible. Artie scampered close behind. Bumshoe threw his back against the rock wall, like James Bond, and even did pistol fingers.

Artie followed suit (not bothering with the pistol fingers), more to please his friend than anything else. From deep inside the cave they could hear faint yapping, squawking, miaowing and hissing noises. But apart from that it was silent. Bending low, Bumshoe poked his head around the corner to look into the cave. He sprang back, his mouth making a perfect 'O' to match the two 'O's of his eyes, and the larger 'O' of his face. Altogether, Bumshoe spelt 'OOOOOOOOO'.

'Wait!' Artie exclaimed. 'Maybe we should just go home ...'

'NO WAY!!!' mouthed his friend excitedly, then crept around the corner and vanished into the gloom.

Artie felt as if his heart was about to bounce right out of his throat and go thumping off across the clearing by itself. He squeezed his eyes tight, as if expecting an explosion, and tore around the corner into the inky black.

Immediately it was clear that the cave was actually a

shallow tunnel and, as Artie's eyes adjusted to the dark, he saw at the back of it a gigantic sliding door, partially ajar, with a wedge of light beyond. The boys scurried through the tunnel, pausing momentarily at the door, and then crept inside.

'COOL! COOL! COOL!'

Bumshoe shout-whispered. *(This, dear reader, is when your face looks like it's shouting but you only let a whisper out.)*

The cave, illuminated by lanterns dangling from the ceiling, opened out into a huge underground space, which was absolutely chock-a-block with incredible stuff …

Motorbikes, kitchen gadgets, car parts, bicycles, sound

systems, TVs, toilet seats, and boxes and boxes, which seemed to be spilling all kinds of jewellery and knick-knacks. But stranger still, against the walls there were rows of cages full of puppies, birds, guinea pigs, rabbits and even a tortoise. The smell was overpowering.

'Must all be stolen stuff! Don't you reckon?' Artie breathed.

Bumshoe nodded solemnly. 'Possibly, quite possibly.' He stopped abruptly as the sound of men's laughter erupted outside the cave.

Artie's blood froze. He strained to listen.

'HawHawHaw.' There it was again.

They tore over to the sliding door and planted their backs against it, James Bond style.

'HawHawHaw.' The laughter was getting closer.

'HawHawHaw.' Two big shapes burst through the doorway. Artie and Bumshoe, stuck fast to the back of the door, were only millimetres away as the figures ambled into the room. Then, as quick and silent as moths, the boys were around the door and bolting across the clearing.

'OI! YOU TWO!' bellowed a voice behind them, but they plunged into the bushes without looking back.

Chapter 3

Wolf!!!

Artie was in trouble. Technically his mum hadn't face-planted, because she was already lying down. Artie's mum, Maggie Small, was lying down most of the time, and always wearing a pale pink dressing-gown. Artie couldn't remember the last time he'd seen her *not* wearing that gown.

She hadn't believed Artie's stories about Nate and Wart, or shoes thrown over power lines, and least of all the Cave-of-Possibly-Stolen-Stuff.

'Please don't make things up, Artie,' said Maggie wearily, looking sideways at her son from the sofa.

'I'm not! It's *true*, Mum,' said the boy.

'Did you leave your shoes somewhere?' she groaned.

'No, Mum! Nate Grime threw them up over power lines … I can show you!' he said, but they both knew that wasn't going to happen, because his mum never went out the front door.

17

'Oh, Artie ...' she said, sounding utterly disappointed.

That was the *worst*. When his mum was *disappointed* it was so much worse than when she completely face-planted or went right off her nut.

He couldn't really blame his mum for not believing him. He was famous for making up big fat porky pies. These were some of Artie's most famous fibs:

1. Telling his mum that scientists in Sweden had discovered the growing brain needed at least three hours of visual stimulation a day to maximise its potential ... so he was under strict instructions to watch more television.
2. Telling his mum that school had been hit by a piece of space debris, and the site had been cordoned off by a Hazardous Chemicals Unit until further notice.
3. Making an appointment with the principal to let him know that he was being sent to boarding school in Switzerland, and so he would no longer be requiring his school's services.

But the most infamous incident was a recent one, when Artie cried ... *wolf*.

It was a winter's night. Artie had just eaten a dinner of baked beans with Lola for the fourth time that week, sitting

in silence as she messaged furiously on her phone. He was
mooching around outside, freezing cold, miserable and bored.
Out of nowhere his heart began pounding madly, and a terrible
feeling of panic overcame him. Before he knew it, he was
hurling himself around in the muddy garden and screaming.

'WOLF!!!! THERE'S A WOLF!!! WOLF!!!!
AAAAARGH, IT'S GOT ME!!!
NOOOO!!! HELP! WOOOOLF!!
WOOLF!!!'

Neighbours from up and down the street began poking their heads out and gawping at the strange spectacle of the loony boy being attacked in his garden by a nonexistent wolf. Then Lola arrived, tugging at her earphones.

'QUIT IT, WILL YOU! STOP BEING SUCH A BONEHEAD AND GET INSIDE!'

Artie still couldn't figure out why he'd done it. Maybe because he was sick of baked beans. Maybe he wanted Lola to put down her phone and talk to him. Or maybe it was because he wanted his mum to come out of her bedroom and cook him something delicious like she used to back in the prehistoric era before his dad died.

Anyway, his wolf escapade definitely hadn't made things better around the Small family home. He only succeeded in making Maggie Small sadder and Lola Small crankier, and Lola was already the crankiest person on earth. Bumshoe tried to cheer Artie up by coming up with ways that Lola's rage could be used by science. 'Eventually,' Bumshoe mused, 'Lola could replace the solid-fuel rocket booster used to launch the space shuttle! They could just lie her down under the shuttle and on the countdown she could yell ARTIE, COME AND EAT YOUR BEANS, YOU MORON! and it'd be off into orbit!'

Needless to say, when she got
home, Lola hadn't believed Artie's
story about the lost shoes either,
let alone the Cave-of-Possibly-
Stolen-Stuff.

'Now I'll have to take you to
the charity shop in the morning
and get you new ones!' she
snapped, glowering at him
over her baked beans.

'I can go by myself,'
said Artie.

'No, you can't', she
shouted. 'Because I've
just paid for the
groceries, so
I'll need to
withdraw more
money and you can't
be trusted to do that
because you're such a turnip!' And
with that she thundered out of the room, slamming the door.

ARTIE, COME AND EAT YOUR BEANS YOU MORON!

Chapter 4

The Cave-of-Almost-Certainly-Stolen-Stuff

The next day Artie woke up late. Lola had already gone out to meet her friends and there was still no money for shoes, so he loitered around the house all day in his bare feet, trying not to think about the Cave-of-Possibly-Stolen-Stuff. Everything about the place gave him a bad feeling in his belly.

Eventually, evening fell, and Artie busied himself making his dinner. Since the night of the wolf he had decided he could never look another baked bean in the eye again, so he had started his own culinary experiments. He knew you couldn't just eat sweet things all the time, so he always tried to add at least one healthy ingredient. Some of his recent feats included:

Tuna Ice-cream Surprise with Sprinkles
Banana, Corn and Spaghetti Smoothie

Nougat and Chocolate Bar Sandwich with Lettuce and Mayonnaise

Carrot, Smarties and Peanut Butter Omelette

Tonight, Artie set about creating a chicken chip, tomato and honey sandwich. He was quietly pleased with the result, having made many worse-tasting sandwiches, and sat alone, munching his creation.

'ARTEEE … ARTEEE …' came a call from outside.

Artie scampered to the kitchen window and saw his neighbour Zoran's face peering over the fence. He put down his sandwich and tore out into the backyard.

'Hi, Zoran!'

Artie's neighbours were a family known as the Unpronounceable-enkos. Their daughter Gladys was in his year at school, and she was always teased about her name and her accent, though Artie really liked both. Gladys was super-bright; in fact she was always coming first in everything. She would often help Artie with his homework, and occasionally, when he was really behind, she would simply give him all the answers, though this was mostly accompanied by a lot of head-shaking and tutting noises.

The Unpronounceable-enkos came from a country called Ukraine. The only part of their name that everyone was certain about was the -enko bit, but the rest of it looked like someone had torn apart a bag of Scrabble tiles. So they were just referred to as the Unpronounceable-enkos.

Artie, however, knew Gladys's full name off by heart, and he would lie in bed practising it, enjoying the feel of the letters rolling around in his mouth … *Gladys Zatserklyannaya-Tsekmistrenko.*

Gladys's mum and dad were always cooking delicious things, and Artie would hang about in his backyard around dinnertime in the hope that he would be invited in.

These dinners were the highlight of Artie's social calendar. Gladys's mum, Oksana, always fussed over him and stroked his hair. She worked as a librarian, and would frequently hand him a book or two that she'd borrowed for him. Zoran was gigantic, hairy and terrifying-looking. He was an Olympic discus champion, and there were photographs of him all over the walls as a young man, wearing Lycra tights and a funny hairdo.

The other good thing about visiting the Unpronounceable-enkos was that Artie would often sit next to Gladys. He never said very much to her, he just liked being around her.

On this particular evening, Zoran looked unusually sombre.

'Hey, Artie. You haven't seen Gareth the tort-oyse, huh?' he whispered.

'Is Gareth missing?' asked Artie.

'Yeah. Very bad, very bad! He been stolen from out of the tank. They steal our telly, and our tort-oyse! You can save up and buy another telly, but there is only one Gareth, you know? Gladys is very upset ...' Zoran gave his huge, hairy head a forlorn shake. 'Anyway, you hungry, Artie?'

'Oh ... maybe ... Just a little bit,' said Artie, whose sandwich didn't seem so appealing anymore.

'Come on, then!' boomed the neighbour. In a flash, Artie had made his way into their yard via the secret passage he'd created through the hedge and was surrounded by the warm mayhem of the Unpronounceable-enko family.

'Where are your shoes, Artie?' asked Oksana, but Artie was saved the embarrassment of answering by Gladys's little twin sisters, who started gabbling stories about their new unicorn shoes.

At the dinner table, Artie noticed that Gladys had been crying. Something felt sore in his chest when he saw that.

'I'm sorry about Gareth,' he said quietly.

'Thanks,' she said. 'Could you please keep a look out for him? Maybe whoever stole him made a mistake. I mean, why would anyone want to steal my tortoise?' Gladys's eyes flooded with tears.

'What's goin' on in the world?' yelled Zoran, 'People all up and down the neighbourhood having things stole from right under them!'

Artie began to feel a prickling sensation on the back of his neck.

'What sort of things?' he asked.

'Everythings! All things!' Zoran bellowed. 'Television, cats, heater, rabbits, clothings ... Who steal clothings? Who steal little girl's tort-oyses?' He glared wild-eyed at Artie, as if *he* was the one who'd been stealing everything.

'Here you go, skinny boy,' said Oksana, laying a huge plate of crumbed meat and vegetables in front of him.

'Have some *this*!' growled Zoran, spearing a great slab of cheese with a knife and waving it in the air. 'I make this cheese myself. With my bare hand!'

Artie had encountered Zoran's cheese before, and knew that even though it smelt like nappies, it tasted absolutely delicious.

In normal circumstances Artie Small would have been blissfully happy in this moment, chewing on the delicious food and listening to the chattering of the Unpronounceable-enkos. But things *weren't* normal. Something bad was going on.

Artie was beginning to think that it had everything to do with the Cave-of-Possibly-Stolen-Stuff, which was now a Cave-of-Almost-Certainly-Stolen-Stuff. He also had an uneasy feeling that whoever the people were at the cave, they must also be responsible for Gareth's disappearance.

As he sat eating his dinner, glancing at Gladys's sad face, Artie made a decision. He would do whatever it took to find her tortoise and bring him safely home.

He almost blurted out the story of the cave, but quickly thought better of it. Why would they believe him? Like the rest of the neighbourhood, the Unpronouceable-enkos had seen him running around his garden being chased by an imaginary wolf.

No, if Artie was going to convince the grown-up world about the cave, he and Bumshoe would need *proof.* And Artie had an idea how to get it ...

Chapter 5

Powder Lollies

The bedrooms at Bumshoe's house looked just like dormitories, with rows of triple-decker bunk beds for all the siblings, and so many clothes and toys strewn over the floors that the floors themselves weren't visible. The boys snuck into one of these rooms and Bumshoe quickly slid open a bedside drawer, pulling out a tiny black object.

'If Angus realises this is gone there'll be *hell* to pay!' he shout-whispered. (*Do you remember about shout-whispering, dear reader?*) 'He saved up for years for this camera!' Artie, who was keeping watch at the bedroom door, didn't really know what 'hell to pay' meant, but it didn't sound good. Bumshoe buried the little object in his pocket in a sticky nest of Chococaramel-Cococreambombs and grinned at his friend.

'Lucky for me our place is so crazy, nobody ever knows where *anything* is!'

As if to prove his point, the bedroom door suddenly burst open and in flew about seven of Bumshoe's siblings, yelling and squirting each other with water pistols. Bumshoe and Artie took the chance to scramble out through the junk of the Bumshoe hallway, past the junk of the Bumshoe lounge room, and beyond the junk of the Bumshoe front yard. They passed about five million Bumshoe brothers and sisters on their way.

So far, Artie's plan was unfolding like clockwork. He had realised that what the pair needed was *video proof,* and he remembered that Bumshoe's brother Angus was always filming animals in the wild, and had the perfect camera for the job. Artie had explained to Bumshoe that if they could just borrow that camera for the weekend, and set it up in exactly the right position in front of the cave, they could film the comings and goings of the robbers. Then they could take the evidence to the police, the robbers would be caught, and last but not least, Artie could return Gareth the tortoise to Gladys, who would be happy once again.

The two boys took off on their bikes, keeping an eagle-eye out for Nate and Wart as they went.

Artie and Bumshoe heard Aunty-boy long before they cycled past her house. There was, as always, a great thumping noise as she pounded out a military march on her piano. Her little ramshackle cottage seemed as if it was about to bounce off its stumps with all the ruckus.

The town was awash with stories about Aunty-boy. Nobody seemed to know how she'd got such a strange name. As long as anyone could remember she had always been Aunty-boy. Some people said she used to be a world-famous concert pianist, and others said she was a mad scientist who only played the piano for relaxation. Others still said she'd had her heart broken when she was a young lady and had lived as a virtual hermit ever since.

What everyone agreed on, though, was that Aunty-boy was NUTS. Stark staring, one hundred per cent, no-shadow-of-a-doubt, let's be clear about it: NUTS. As nutty as a plate of peanuts if you took the peas away. Or a plate of walnuts if you took the walls away. Or a plate of Brazil nuts if you took Brazil away. She was just plain *nuts*.*

* *Please note, dear reader : this sentence may contain nuts*

As the boys rode past her house, the piano abruptly stopped, the window flew open, and the old lady popped her head out.

'Yikes. Yikes. Boys on bikes!' she chirped. 'Where are you headed, butterscotch pies?'

Aunty-boy was about the same size across as she was up and down. Always wearing brightly coloured clothing, she looked a bit like somebody's balloon collection. She wore thick spectacles, which gave the impression that she was gazing at you through the bottom of drinking glasses, and kept her white hair up in a tight little bun. She clacked her false teeth out at the two boys and said, 'Wait, wait! Sweeties for sweeties!'

The boys waited while they heard the old lady unbolting the multiple locks on her door. Then she burst out with her dog, Macaroni, offering the boys lollies from a paper bag. They clambered off their bikes and patted the animal, who squirmed excitedly around their legs. Macaroni looked as if he was made entirely of spare parts from other dogs, but he adored his mistress, and was highly intelligent.

Artie and Bumshoe *dreaded* being offered sweets by Aunty-boy. The problem was this: Aunty-boy never, *ever* had a bath or shower, instead choosing to fling baby powder over herself each night before bed. Over the years, every single surface in Aunty-boy's house had become coated in a thick layer of powder, including her gigantic stash of lollies, which looked like they'd been uncovered in an archeological dig. When eating one of the old lady's sweets, Artie could never escape the thought that he was also tasting the powder that had once replaced a bath or shower, possibly twenty or thirty years before …

Artie himself had a fairly relaxed attitude to personal hygiene (without a parent there to insist, he could sometimes forget about showering for days on end), but Aunty-boy was vehemently opposed to the whole idea of soap and water, and railed against it. Today, unprompted, she launched into a little poem on the subject, bobbing up and down, flapping her arms and chanting.

Being very polite boys, Artie and Bumshoe would always accept the stale and powder-coated objects, pop them in their mouths, hold their breath and feign immense enjoyment. Then, once safely out of sight, they would eject the hideous mouthfuls with much hacking and spitting.

One time Artie tried to sneak one of these ghastly morsels to Macaroni, assuming the dog would be thrilled. But even

Ain't got webbed feet
Ain't got scales ◦ you oughta
keep away from me with your cold wet water!
A little puff of talc is the thing for grannies
To keep clean as a whistle their nooks and crannies

Macaroni sniffed at the gooey mess on the pavement and turned away in disgust.

Today, as ever, the boys dutifully accepted a lolly each.

'Mmmm,' they said in unison. 'Delicious.'

'Where are you buzzing to, cherry strudels?' asked Aunty-boy.

'Up Nail Can Hill,' said Artie.

'Ooooh. That's a big trip. Big trip. Toodle-pip!' said Aunty-boy, clacking her dentures out again for effect. 'And look out, look out! Strange folk about! Persons unknown tried to steal my Macaroni and put him in a van yesterday! Didn't they, boy?' she cried, bending down and talking directly to the dog, who thumped his tail delightedly in agreement. Artie exchanged a look of concern with Bumshoe.

'You'll need provisions! Energy, boys, energy!' carolled Aunty-boy, and with this she offered the bag of lollies again.

'Thanks, Aunty-boy, but we've probably got enough energy now,' said Bumshoe.

'Quick, boys, quick! Grab a handful! Sweeties for sweeties,' she chortled.

Reluctantly, the boys dipped into the powdery mess and pulled out more of the fossilised sweets.

At that moment, Nate and his gang appeared down the road. In a flash Artie and Bumshoe were off on their bikes, calling thanks to Aunty-boy over their shoulders. Safely out of sight, they spat their lollies as far as they could, and kept spitting until the taste of powder was finally gone.

Chapter 6

The boys soon found their way back up to the cave. Having been spotted by the robbers last time, today they took care not to make a sound. They slid down gently through the bushes towards the clearing. Artie was extra careful as he still had no shoes, and his feet were spiked with prickles and sticks at every step.

Today the place was abuzz with activity. There was a van in the clearing as well as a huge black motorbike with a sidecar. Some scary-looking men were coming and going, carrying all manner of objects that the boys were now fully convinced were stolen.

One of the men carried a cage of brilliant-coloured birds in one hand and yapping puppies in the other.

'Check that out! This has got to be where poor old Gareth ended up,' exclaimed Bumshoe under his breath.

Artie and Bumshoe wasted no time getting to work. The plan was to position the tiny camera and film the gang of robbers over one entire day. The camera was motion-activated, so it would only record when people were arriving and transporting things to and from the cave. The boys would return the following day and go straight to the police station with their video evidence.

Having chosen the perfect tree for the task, Bumshoe crouched down and Artie clambered onto his shoulders. On the count of three, Bumshoe grunted and raised himself upright.

From there, Artie was able to haul himself into the fork of the tree. Despite the fact that his dad had been a trapeze artist and tightrope walker, Artie was terrified of heights. His heart was galloping. To make matters worse, he suddenly realised he was completely exposed to the clearing below. Why was he doing this? This was exactly the kind of thing he *hated*! An adventure ... and a terrifying one at that! He wished more than anything that he was brave like his dad, but he wasn't. He froze. If the gang spied him now, who knew what would happen?

Then Artie thought of Gladys, and how thoroughly

miserable she looked without her tortoise. He reached forward and jammed the camera into a small flat shelf between two branches, making sure it pointed at the entrance to the cave.

'Don't forget to turn it on!' yell-whispered Bumshoe from below.

Artie clicked the little green button and the tiny camera pinged on. Now they would have *proof*!

At that moment, a huge black car came roaring into the clearing below and slid to a halt. Two enormous men in black suits and sunglasses sprang out and opened the back door, then stood to attention as a man in a shiny blue suit emerged. He had long, sparse strands of hair slicked down over a balding scalp. He stood with his back to Artie and began barking orders at the thieves, who immediately came running.

Artie was trapped in full view and only metres away from the group. He stayed deathly still. Sweat started trickling down from the top of his head into his eyes. *Maybe they'll think I'm a koala*, he thought. He tried to think koala-like thoughts to calm his pounding heart.

'YOU'RE DAWDLING!' bellowed the man below. 'YOU'VE ALL GOT TO WORK FASTER! DO YOU THINK IT'S THE WEEKEND OR SOMETHING?'

One of the thieves, a wispy little man who was clutching a cage of chirping finches, murmured, 'Well, it is the weekend, Boss ...'

'WHAT DID YOU SAY?' screamed the man.

'Erm ... Well, it is Sunday, and that is ... um ... the weekend ... technically, Boss,' said the thief.

The man in the suit clicked his fingers, and one of the men in sunglasses lurched forward, plucked the cage from the thief's hands, lifted it high in the air and smashed it down over the little man's head. Startled finches flitted away in all directions.

The man in sunglasses, expressionless, stepped back to re-join his colleague at attention.

'What day of the week is it?'

'Erm ... Not Sunday?' said the thief.

'That's right,' said the man. 'It's not Sunday until I say it's Sunday. Is it?'

'Is it?' said the little voice from inside the birdcage.

'Is what *what*?' fumed the man.

'Is it Sunday? Are you saying it's Sunday?'

'NO! THAT'S WHAT I'VE BEEN SAYING!'

'Right,' said the tiny voice from inside the cage. 'Just checking …'

'WHY IS IT SO HARD TO FIND GOOD HELP NOWADAYS?' screamed the man in the suit, turning to the others. 'YOU KNOW, THEFT USED TO BE A *NOBLE* PROFESSION! THERE WAS RESPECT! THIEVES TOOK A BIT OF PRIDE IN THEIR WORK! BUT NOW … OH, NO! THERE'S NO RESPECT FOR THE BOSS … EVERYBODY'S JUST IN IT FOR THEMSELVES! WHERE ARE YOUR MORALS?!'

He glanced about, looking for support. In exasperation, he clicked his fingers at the men in sunglasses, who immediately began shaking their heads and making 'tsk, tsk, tsk' noises.

'Alright, that's enough!' he barked impatiently, turning back to the little man.

'You're going to keep this cage on your head until I say you can take it off,' he seethed. 'As a little reminder to work faster, and of who the *boss* is, Mr Budgie.'

At this the other thieves snickered.

'WHAT ARE YOU LAUGHING AT? GET TO WORK OR YOU'LL ALL BE

WEARING BIRDCAGES!' The man stared hard at the group, which scattered like mice, and Artie could see his face clearly for the first time. His eyes were unnaturally small, almost invisible, and something about him seemed oddly familiar.

Miraculously failing to notice the boy pretending to be a koala up a nearby tree, the boss stomped back to his car. One of the men in sunglasses opened the door for him as the other climbed into the driver's seat. In an instant, they were gone. Artie slid down, landing with a thud on Bumshoe, who flew face-first into the dirt.

'Sorry!' whispered Artie.

'Don't worry,' grinned Bumshoe, spitting out some dust. 'Did you see who the boss is?'

'Who?' said Artie.

'THE MAYOR!' Bumshoe scream-whispered.

Artie sat staring at his friend, open-mouthed.

'Nate's dad!' Bumshoe continued. 'IT'S MAYOR GRIME!!'

Chapter 7

Graystains

It was Monday. Artie's least favourite day of the week. This Monday felt different though, because after school, he and Bumshoe were going to retrieve Angus's camera and catch a gang of robbers. Over-excited, he had tossed and turned all night. Now he had to somehow get through the awful, endless, dreary day of school.

But Artie still had no shoes. Realising that he wouldn't be allowed at school in that state, he was at a loss, until he had a brainwave.

He waited until he heard the front door slam as Lola left for school (there was never any doubt about this moment, because when his eternally furious sister slammed doors they nearly blew out of their frames). He found a box of old paints, took them into the bathroom, lay down on the floor and coated his feet top and bottom with a thick layer of black. Then, still lying with his feet in the air, Artie reached for Lola's hair dryer and blew them dry.

Artie stood and inspected his handiwork. Hopefully:

1. Nobody would notice.
2. It wouldn't rain.

Artie's school was an unrelentingly dreary place of concrete and demountable classrooms. As if being a Monday wasn't bad enough, Artie had a double maths class on Monday afternoons. His worst nightmare, double maths meant twice the amount of Mr Graystains, the most boring teacher in the galaxy, or indeed any outlying galaxies, and possibly the entire universe (although Artie realised this was difficult to independently confirm).

Mr Graystains was very tall and very thin. He spoke quietly in a monotonous drone that sounded like a mosquito trapped in a spider web in a faraway land. His hair at some point had retreated from his head and started coming out of his nostrils instead. He also had a World Championship Adam's apple. This, combined with his sudden darting movements, gave Artie the impression of an unhappy emu.

On this particular Monday, Mr Graystains seemed

especially unhappy.

'I'll have no nonsense today of any shape or form,' he intoned. 'Someone has burgled my house over the weekend and made off with my abacus collection, as well as my two beloved Mexican walking fish, so I'm not in any mood for hijinks or hoo-ha.'

At the mention of the robbery Artie locked eyes with Gladys, who, reminded of the loss of Gareth, looked scared and sad. Mr Graystains's news was further confirmation of Artie and Bumshoe's theory about the cave. An icy chill ran down the boy's spine.

The hours of maths dragged endlessly by, and Artie gazed out the window, hearing the distant mosquito hum of Mr Graystains: '… bzzzzz … integers … bzzzzz … prime number … bzzzzz … fraction … bzzzz … square root … your shoes!!!!'

'Wha—?'

With an awful jolt Artie realised that his shoulder was being shaken by Mr Graystains. He'd drifted off to sleep, his head on the desk, dreaming of the Cave-of-Possibly-But-Now-Almost-Definitely-Stolen-Stuff.

'Where are your *shoes*, I said?' demanded Mr Graystains. 'Is this a joke? How dare you sleep in my classroom, and how dare you go barefoot in this school!'

Artie stared vacantly at the incensed teacher, whose face was millimetres from his, and whose breath was like warm gusts of air from a Tupperware container in which something had gone off a great many years ago.

The other students began trying to look at Artie's feet, and an uncontrollable whoop of laughter spread around the room like a bushfire.

'Silence!' hissed Mr Graystains.

Artie felt his cheeks burning. He squeezed his mouth into a tight line, which was his trick to stop crying, and caught sight of Gladys, who was gazing at him sadly.

'Detention for you tomorrow lunchtime!!' breathed Mr Graystains.

PPPPRRRRRIIINGGGGGG.

The school bell rang. The beautiful bell! The best bell in the whole wide world! How Artie loved the bell at that moment. He wanted to kiss that bell. To marry it. To take it away on a honeymoon!

At last he was free on his bike, tearing along with Bumshoe up to the cave to complete their secret mission. They detoured via the charity shop so that Artie could run inside and find some shoes.

Nearing Aunty-boy's street, they heard the customary thumping of the piano, but they turned earlier than usual, to avoid being spotted by her. There was no time for fun – today they were on serious business. Also, the idea of more ancient powder lollies made their gizzards churn.

At long last they were picking their way down through the bush towards the cave. A car, a van and the gigantic motorbike with a sidecar were parked in the clearing, but everything seemed mysteriously quiet.

The stench emanating from the toilet pit seemed to be particularly hideous today, which made their eyes water.

Bumshoe turned to Artie and waggled his hand backwards and forwards over his nose to give the internationally recognised signal for 'stench'. He then knelt down to give Artie a boost up into the tree.

Artie quickly shimmied along the branch to the exact spot he'd left the camera …

It was gone.

Panicking, he looked around to see if he'd made a mistake. But there was no doubt. The little hollow where he'd left the camera was empty!

'IT'S NOT HERE!' Artie shout-whispered.

'WHAT?' Bumshoe shout-whispered in reply.

'THE CAMERA. IT'S NOT HERE!' Artie shout-whispered again.

'Is this what you're looking for?' came a deep and raspy voice from right beside them.

A small shrub was thrust aside at the toilet pit, revealing a gigantic bald man. He was holding the boys' camera in the air with one hand, and was struggling to pull up his trousers with the other. At least they knew now what that terrible stench was.

Covering the man's entire face was a tattoo, which read:

The stench! The spelling mistakes! It was all too much for the boys, who froze like statues. The man gave an evil snicker.

'OI!! FELLAS! I'VE CAUGHT THEM!' he bellowed. Dark figures began to emerge from the cave.

'COME ON, YOU IDIOTS!' he screamed. 'I'M TRYING TO GET MY PANTS UP!'

Artie and Bumshoe, snapping out of their stupor, sprang to life. Artie dived straight out of the tree onto his friend's shoulders, causing Bumshoe to stagger directly into the man.

'Ah … Ahhh … AHHHHH,' moaned the gigantic man, trying desperately to maintain his balance. But with his pants around his ankles, he tripped and plummeted backwards right into the pit with a nasty-sounding SPLAT.

Horrified, the boys didn't linger to see what had just happened, but turned and flew up the hill.

Chapter 8

MARY

The boys scarcely took a breath as they scrambled up over the hill and down the other side to where they had hidden their bikes. They didn't utter a word but jumped on board and tore off down the hill.

Finally they allowed themselves a moment to exchange a look.

'Wow!' said Artie. 'I'd like to never see *him* again!'

'**Mary**,' chuckled Bumshoe. 'Do you reckon he's realised his face is full of spelling mistakes?' The boys giggled, relieved to have escaped, but then Bumshoe's face clouded over. 'What do we do about Angus's camera?' he said. The boys pondered their situation and at last slowed to a more leisurely pace.

FUDFUDFUDFUDFUD

Rounding the bend right behind them was Mary, on the
enormous motorbike with a sidecar. His tumble into the toilet
pit had left him a very unpleasant colour. He had a giant whip,
and upon spying the boys he cracked it, making a noise like a
gunshot as he roared towards them on his machine. He looked
very, **very**, very cranky.

In a shower of stones and dust, Mary was upon them, and
grabbed hold of Artie's arm.

Bumshoe, cycling on the other side of Mary, screamed,
'RABBITS!!!'

The huge man, confused, turned to face him, but oversteered, letting go of Artie's arm. He skidded off the road at high speed and ploughed into a ditch. In an instant the boys abandoned their bikes and ran into the thick bush at the side of the track. Scurrying up the hill through the undergrowth, they found a dense thicket of ferns where they crouched silent and still, their hearts hammering in their chests.

Far below through the trees they could glimpse Mary hunched over with his bottom in the air as he cursed and tried to haul his bike out of the ditch.

The big man turned and scanned the bushes all around, trying to catch sight of them. He flicked his whip for effect, letting out a monstrous WHAPPAT!!! The sound echoed up and down the valley.

Artie and Bumshoe ducked even lower into the foliage. Soon they heard a roaring noise followed by a terrible crunching. The boys ventured a peek. Mary had managed to haul his machine out of the ditch, and was now riding it back and forth over the top of their bicycles, squishing them and smashing them to pieces. Artie gasped. It had been bad enough when he'd arrived home with no shoes. He couldn't imagine how his mum was going to react when he turned up with no bicycle!

'OH, SORRY, BOYS,' Mary cried. 'I DIDN'T SEE THOSE BIKES THERE! WHOOPSIE! OH NO, DIDN'T SEE THEM AGAIN! CLUMSY ME!'

Not succeeding in rousing the boys from their hiding place, Mary yelled, 'OI! DON'T YOU WANT YOUR CAMERA BACK, BOYS?' He gave a snigger and held the little object high above his head. 'NICE LITTLE CAMERA! FINDERS KEEPERS, I GUESS!'

Artie, mortified, stared at Bumshoe, who shrugged and shook his head.

Mary gave a lingering look up the hill, trying to see any sign of the boys, then, fuming, flung the camera into the sidecar.

FUDFUDFUDFUDFUD

The gigantic man rode up and down the track until it was almost dark, yelling threats and cracking his whip.

WHAPPAT!! WHAPPAT!! WHAPPAT!!

Artie and Bumshoe stayed buried among the bushes, sneaking an occasional glimpse at the road, until at last they heard the motorbike retreating up the hill.

Artie gazed forlornly at his friend. Ruined bikes, lost camera, no proof, and their secret ploy uncovered. This day was not turning out as planned …

Thunder cracked across the sky and rain began to fall in big fat drops.

Chapter 9

SIDECAR

Artie and Bumshoe scampered over to a rock shelf, crouching underneath to shelter from the storm. Bumshoe offered some Chococaramel-Cococreambombs and they sat munching for a while, contemplating their predicament.

'What do we do now?' said Artie.

'I can't go home without that camera,' said Bumshoe. 'Angus will go *ballistic*.'

'And what about the proof?' said Artie. 'Gladys will never see Gareth again.'

'Well. We saw Mary throw the camera into his sidecar,' mused Bumshoe. 'My bet is it's still there.'

'But we can't go back up again! What if they're lying in wait for us?' exclaimed Artie, who felt that he'd had enough adventures to last him until he was at least as old as Mr Graystains.

'They'll never expect us to turn up at the cave again!' said Bumshoe. 'We'd have to be *mental* to do that! Don't you see, it's the perfect plan!' With a triumphant grin he was up, brushing Chococaramel-Cococreambomb crumbs off his pants.

Artie was horrified at the thought of confronting the gang once again.

'Can't we just sell something and get enough money to buy Angus a new camera?' he ventured.

'What are we going to sell?' Bumshoe asked. 'All I've got at my place is a whole lot of junk and piles of brothers and sisters.' After a moment he added, 'S'pose I could sell one of them. Nobody'd really notice …' He chuckled grimly.

Artie knew his friend was right. The only thing he owned that was worth anything was his bicycle, which now lay squished beyond recognition on the track below. The boys wandered down and sadly inspected the remains.

'Well, I guess we've got nothing to lose now,' sighed Artie. And with that, the two boys trudged back up the hill in the rain.

By the time they reached the cave night had fallen. They crouched in the bushes again and gazed at the scene below. The clearing was floodlit and the cars and vans were still parked outside. Right near the entrance to the cave sat Mary's gigantic motorbike and sidecar.

A skinny man wearing a filthy black T-shirt, black braces and black jeans was carrying objects from the back of a van into the cave. Artie noticed that one of these objects was a small fish tank. He briefly wondered if it contained Mr Graystains's beloved Mexican walking fish. Mary suddenly emerged and yelled, 'OI, FUNNEL-WEB, DID YOU PUT THAT TV IN THE SOUND SYSTEM SECTION?'

'SO WHAT IF I DID?' growled the skinny man. The boys suddenly saw that the man's face was covered in hair, and that he had filed all his teeth to sharp little points. He looked horribly, as his name suggested, like a funnel-web spider.

'YOU KNOW THE BOSS HATES MESS!' shouted Mary.

'AIN'T SCARED OF HIM!' croaked Funnel-web.

'Well, you should be scared … Look what he's done to me!' called a voice from behind Mary, and out of the shadows emerged the little robber, still wearing the birdcage on his head.

Funnel-web emitted an awful rasping cackle. 'HAHAHA.'

'Not funny!' said the little face from inside the birdcage.

'Actually, it is pretty funny!' whispered Bumshoe to Artie.

'HAHAHA,' gasped
Funnel-web. 'Does
Mr Budgie want a
cracker?'

'Not funny,
I said!' cried the
man in the
birdcage.
'You won't
be laughing
when the
boss makes

you wear one of these on your head.'

But the angrier Mr Budgie became the funnier the other thieves found it, and soon Funnel-web and Mary were falling about with laughter.

'RIGHT!' gasped Mary abruptly. 'ENOUGH MUCKING ABOUT! BACK TO WORK! AND KEEP AN EYE OUT FOR THOSE NOSY BOYS! AND FUNNEL-WEB, A TV IS NOT A SOUND SYSTEM, ORRIGHT?!'

Funnel-web, muttering under his breath, sploshed through

the rain with a large box, and the motley bunch disappeared into the cave.

'Okay,' sighed Bumshoe. 'I guess this is the moment ...'

Artie took a deep breath. As much as he hated adventures, his concern for Bumshoe outweighed his fears for himself. He stood up.

'Bumshoe,' he whispered. 'I'll go and get it.'

But Bumshoe merely patted his friend on the shoulder and gazed at him earnestly. 'Look and learn, my friend. Look and learn.'

He wriggled his eyebrows and bolted down through the scrub, straight out into the clearing. He was completely exposed under the floodlights. If anyone came out of the cave now, all would be lost.

Artie crouched, terrified, and watched as his friend arrived at Mary's motorbike and began trying to tear back the cover on the sidecar.

This seemed to take an unbearable amount of time. In his head Artie was shouting, 'HURRY UP!!!' But Bumshoe was clearly struggling with the rubber cover. Artie stood, and was just about to run over and help, when at last his friend clawed the cover back and reached inside.

Bumshoe turned, beaming, and kissed the camera, then lifted it high in the air, first to one side and then the other, like a Formula One driver parading a trophy on a podium.

STOP GOOFING AROUND! Artie thought, and had begun signalling urgently at him to come back when the robbers poured out of the cave. The awful man called Funnelweb had a gigantic animal on a leash, a sort of zombie-dog, which immediately began baying and thrashing about.

Artie watched in horror as Bumshoe dived headfirst into the sidecar, hauling the cover over himself. The thief had not seen Bumshoe, but the enormous animal was barking uncontrollably, baring its giant fangs, with slobber flying everywhere, trying to get to the sidecar.

'SHUT UP, TINKERBELL, WHAT'S THE MATTER WITH YOU, YOU NAUGHTY BOY?' growled Funnel-web, and he dragged the hound away, shoved it into the back of the car and roared off down the track. *Since when is Tinkerbell a boy?* thought Artie.

Mary lurched over, mounted his bike and gunned it to life. Artie watched helplessly as he circled the clearing and tore off down the track, spraying mud everywhere – his unknown cargo trapped in the sidecar right beside him.

Meanwhile, Mr Budgie finished loading some televisions into the van. He clambered inside and began to manoeuvre it around in the mud.

Artie peered desperately at the van.

At the back of it there was a little metal foot grille and a door handle. Before he had time to think, he sprinted through the rain and leapt up onto the step, grabbing hold of the handle. The van sped up, splashing and thudding down the track, trying to keep up with the others. Stricken with fear and sprayed all over with mud, Artie clung on for his life.

Chapter 10

New Friends

Artie was relieved when the drive down the bumpy, muddy track of Nail Can Hill finally ended and they were on a proper sealed road. But his relief was short-lived: the van started speeding up, until it was rocketing through the dark streets of the town. They skidded around corners and overtook cars. Artie gripped the door handle so tightly he thought he might go flying off and actually leave his hands behind.

Finally, the van slowed as they entered a dingy industrial suburb and turned up a dark side street. Ahead, Artie could hear the FUDFUDFUD of Mary's motorbike slowing to a halt. The van stopped alongside a huge old factory with a high razorwire fence. There was a checkpoint at the gate, and two security guards with pistols on their belts.

The moment the van braked, Artie jumped down and sprinted to some bushes on the far side of the road. From this vantage point he watched as Funnel-web's car and Mary's bike crept forwards and stopped at the security gate. The two robbers began chatting and laughing with the sentries. Artie hoped frantically that the guards wouldn't think to pull back the cover of Mary's sidecar.

Somehow, he was going to have to get into the compound, rescue Bumshoe, and escape! But how could he get past the checkpoint? He obviously couldn't jump onto the back of the van again. Even though he looked like a giant mud-patty after his journey, he'd be spotted immediately.

Think! Think! Think! Artie held his forehead. *Why can't I be brave and strong like my dad was? He would never have let a problem like this beat him! He would have…Well, what would he have done?* thought Artie. *He would probably have just run over to that tree near the gate, and climbed straight up it, and then dropped down onto the roof of Mr Budgie's van to catch a lift past the guards without being spotted…*

Artie thought no more. He ran as silently as possible across the darkened street, until he arrived at the trunk of the tree. Mary and Funnel-web had finished chatting with the guards and were now moving the motorbike and car into the compound. With a jolt, Mr Budgie's van began trundling along behind. Artie had only seconds to spare!

He climbed up the base of the tree and, like a leopard, scrabbled out onto the long limb that dangled over the road. The branch bent alarmingly under his weight. As the van moved forward underneath him, he slid a tiny bit further, and the limb bowed even more, and began to crack!

Just as it seemed about to snap off and send him plummeting, the branch gracefully deposited Artie onto the roof of the van without so much as a thump. He let go and it twanged back up into the air. *Wow...Cool!* he thought, allowing a rare moment of self-congratulation as he lay splayed on the roof. *And I didn't even have time to be scared by the height!*

Unseen by the gatekeepers, the boy on the roof breathed a sigh of relief as the van was waved straight through into the dingy compound. With a scraping of metal doors, the convoy lurched forward into the factory itself. Artie rolled onto his stomach and peered about. The building was gargantuan, and completely full of cars, equipment, thousands of boxes overflowing with stolen booty and hundreds of animals in cages. Dozens of workers were loading and unloading objects, zipping about on forklift trucks.

Artie looked about in disbelief. There were walls of TVs, fridges, computers, jewellery and paintings, all neatly stacked into sections. Teams of men were pulling cars apart and spraying them new colours. Other groups were pulling stolen computers and electronic equipment to pieces.

They're changing the serial numbers on everything to resell it on the black market! thought Artie.

The van ground to a halt, and Artie heard Mr Budgie get out and slam the door. Somewhere in the building he heard the awful barking and howling of the zombie-dog. He wriggled to the edge of the roof and peered over, but could see no sign of Mary's bike. Mr Budgie, still wearing his birdcage, had plopped himself nearby on a pile of chairs as workers began unloading the van. He opened the door to his birdcage and began excavating his nose with a finger.

Artie squirmed his way over to the other side of the van and peeked around that edge. A sofa had been deposited directly below. Right beside it was Mary's bike – but the sidecar was uncovered and completely empty! Artie's heart began pounding, his breath coming in ragged gasps. Had the gang caught Bumshoe? Suddenly, way above Artie's head, a gantry door was flung open and out of an office emerged Funnel-web and Mary. Mary was making a joke, and Funnel-web, his thumbs hooked into his braces, was doubled over with laughter.

Artie, sprawled on the roof of the van, was now clearly visible. Against all his instincts and horror of heights, he squeezed his eyes shut and let himself roll over the edge, plummeting onto the sofa below. Incredulous that he was still alive and apparently intact, he wriggled under the cushions.

Immediately, he was aware of the sofa being lifted, and was taken on a jolting ride.

'Feels heavier than it did a second ago,' an unknown voice grumbled.

'End of the day ...' complained another. 'Things always feel heavier. Not getting paid enough for all this.'

Artie felt the sofa dumped hard onto the ground, and the two workers grumbled off into the distance. Venturing a look, he realised he was in a dimly lit section at the back of the factory, surrounded by furniture, white goods and musical instruments.

Directly to the side of him lay a great hill of washing machines and dryers. And there, right at the very top of the pile, his head poking out from under a washing machine lid, was Bumshoe! Artie could barely contain his excitement.

'PSSSST! PSSSST!' he hissed.

Bumshoe spun around, and spying Artie, he beamed. But his sudden movement had set the machine wobbling. Overbalancing, it began to teeter and, as if in slow motion, started tumbling all the way to the bottom, gathering momentum as it went.

BOM

BOM

BOM

BOM

BOM

Bom   bombombombomb-b-b-b-b-b

Silence

The mangled machine sat right in the middle of the aisle. Slowly the lid squeaked open and Bumshoe's head poked out like a turtle's. Artie could only watch from his hiding place, appalled, as he saw Funnel-web turn and begin clattering down the stairs from the gantry.

'Well, well, well,' croaked the spidery man. 'Looks like we've got a little spy on our hands.'

In seconds, Bumshoe was surrounded by a small crowd of factory workers. They parted as Funnel-web stepped in closer to the boy, followed by Mr Budgie.

'He looks a little grubby, fellas,' leered Funnel-web, his sharpened teeth glinting in the light. 'Maybe we should fire up that washing machine and run him through a couple of cycles!'

'BRING HIM UP HERE,' said a voice that sent a shiver down Artie's spine. Slowly lifting the sofa cushion higher, Artie saw Mary's tattooed face gazing down from the shadows of the gantry. 'We love making new friends ...'

Chapter 11

Bungee~Wedgie

Artie watched, mortified, as the crowd dragged his friend out of the battered washing machine. Bumshoe, who looked transfixed with fear, stared at the floor.

'HOLD ON A BIT!' growled Mary from above. 'I believe I've already met our chubby little friend! He's one of the sneaky brats who's been sniffing around the cave trying to film us. You've made our boss very angry, boy!' he snarled down at Bumshoe, but then turned to the crowd. 'But when I was chasing him, he had a little friend with him. A scrawny little squirt. I'm betting he's here somewhere as well!'

Artie gasped in fear. His mind was doing somersaults.

Funnel-web turned to the little man with the birdcaged head. 'Oi, Mr Budgie, get Tinkerbell out of my car. He'll sniff him out in a jiffy!'

'Stop calling me that! And why am I the one who has to get

Tinkerbell?' grizzled Mr Budgie. 'I hate Tinkerbell ...'

'Awww. He won't hurt you,' smirked Funnel-web. 'It's cats who eat budgies, not dogs!' At this he burst into wild guffaws, joined by the crowd of workers and Mary on the gantry above.

'Not funny!' cried the voice from inside the birdcage.

'Why are we all laughing then, Mr Budgie?' called Mary.

Artie watched helplessly as Bumshoe was frogmarched up to the gantry, and the little robber with the birdcage on his head set off to fetch the terrible animal. Artie was panicking. In seconds, the monstrous zombie-dog would be unleashed and tearing him to pieces!

Once again, Artie berated himself. *Why couldn't I have been born brave, like Dad?* he thought. *Or even just smart? Smart would be good! If I was smart and brave like Dad, I'd know exactly what to do. I mean, in a situation like this, Dad would just ... well, he would ... probably just ...* GET OUT OF HERE!

All activity in the factory stopped, as groups of workers began patrolling about trying to find Artie. It was a matter of minutes before he would be discovered. With nothing to lose, he lifted the cushion a bit higher and looked wildly about. Way up high on the back wall he spied a window, and below, leading all the way up to it, was a sort of staircase of musical instruments. In the other direction, towards the front of the factory, was a mountain of cardboard boxes. If he could just distract everyone for a minute! Right beside him, in a box of stolen junk, he spied a rubber chicken. *Why would someone steal a rubber chicken?* Artie thought. *I mean, really, how much are they going to get for a second-hand rubber chicken?*

Then, scolding himself for wasting precious time with irrelevant thoughts, he grabbed the chicken by the neck, sprang up, and with all the strength he could summon, he flung it as far as he could towards the pile of cardboard boxes.

The chicken walloped one of the boxes at the top, and they all began to tumble, spilling their contents and making a huge clamour. The workers spun around and sprinted towards the noise.

Meanwhile, Artie darted in the opposite direction and began clambering up over the mound of grand pianos, guitars, drum kits, piano accordions and glockenspiels. The noise was cacophonous!

GROOONG!

FIDDDIDID!

WHAAACK!

BOOOOSH!

THRUMMM!

PLAANG!

PLIIING!

BOOOOM!

PAAARP!

It sounded like a symphony that might have been composed by Aunty-boy. Artie hoisted himself up onto a xylophone, its wooden bars tumbling everywhere. At last reaching the window, he tried to yank it open. *It was stuck fast!*

Below him the factory workers, realising they'd been tricked, were now attempting to scramble up behind him. But being much heavier and clumsier than Artie, they kept plummeting through kettledrums, smashing violins and double basses, and falling back to the ground.

GROOOOOOWRRRRR!!!!!

It was Tinkerbell! Artie spun around and saw the fiendish animal bounding up the hill of instruments, its eyes narrowed into yellow slits, its mouth pulled back to reveal a huge expanse of blood-red gums and razor-sharp teeth.

Artie tore at the window, but it wouldn't budge! The hound was gaining on him. It snapped its jaws open and sprang right at him. He closed his eyes, giving in to his final fate as a doggie snack. But the awful animal, attempting to land on the xylophone, sent more bars tumbling off the instrument, lost its footing, and with an almighty

BOOOM
THUNK
KLANG
PRING

WHOMP

it shot out of sight between some oboes and a tuba and disappeared down into the musical mountain.

Artie once again yanked at the window, which started to rattle. But from nowhere, a bony hand grasped his leg like a clamp. It was Funnel-web, who had scuttled up the hill like a spider.

'Come on, little fella,' he murmured. 'We won't hurt you. Just want a chat.' His smile displayed the row of sharpened teeth, and he tightened his grip on Artie's leg.

With a supreme final effort, Artie prised the window open. A gust of cold air blew in his face and he leant out. It was only then that he realised he was *two storeys up from the footpath outside!* He instinctively leant backwards, accidentally grabbing on to the elastic braces holding up Funnel-web's trousers. Then, falling away from the hairy man, he tumbled clear out the window, clinging tight to the braces. Artie was sure he was going to die, but just as he was about to crash to the ground, he sprang right back up, like a bungee jumper!

As he bounced he saw Funnel-web trapped with his head out the window and his trousers dragged all the way up to his armpits! Artie realised that each time he fell he was giving Funnel-web a humungous wedgie!

Meanwhile Tinkerbell, who was back again, had apparently found an irresistible target, and was chomping and tearing at its master's bottom.

'OOOOOOOOWWW ... MY BUM! MY BUM!' screamed Funnel-web. 'GET HIM OFF ME!!'

But the factory workers, terrified of the hideous beast, seemed to be scrambling away in all other directions.

Artie grabbed his opportunity. The next time he dipped down, he let go of the braces and landed with a thud on the pavement below.

Right beside him was a massive pile of stolen bicycles. He grabbed the first one he saw (which happened to be a hot-pink girls' bike with little lilac flag on the back) and took off like a rocket, straight towards the checkpoint. Artie felt sick at leaving Bumshoe behind, but he knew that right now the only hope of rescuing him was to escape.

The security guards, completely bewildered by the vision of a skinny boy cycling out of the compound on a girls' bike, stared at him open-mouthed.

'RABBITS!!!' Artie yelled, and gave a little *ting* on his bell.

This confused them even more, and Artie flew straight past on his rickety bike. *Bumshoe's good old rabbit trick*, he thought. *Works every time!*

He tore off down the dingy street, but behind him he heard angry shouting, the sound of car engines, and the distinct and ominous FUDFUDFUDFUDFUD of Mary's motorbike roaring to life …

Chapter 12

The River

Artie needed a plan. His little pink bike was no match for a car and motorbike. He belted down the long road surrounded by wet, empty yards and falling-down warehouses, which looked gloomy and sinister in the moonlight.

He heard the furious roar of the car tearing up behind him and was suddenly trapped in the glare of its headlights. Up ahead he spied a steep set of concrete stairs descending into muddy flatlands. Artie knew the area vaguely from explorations with Bumshoe. He knew that somewhere down in the dark beyond the marsh must be the river that weaved its way through the town. At the very last moment he threw his bike into a turn and thudded down the stairway.

He reached the bottom and took off across the boggy paddock. Glancing over his shoulder, he saw that the cars had stopped at the top, and Funnel-web and Mr Budgie were now running down the stairs on foot. But all at once they leapt out of the way as Mary came clattering down the staircase between them on his motorbike.

Skidding and slipping in the mire, Artie found himself being chased for the second time by Mary on a motorbike! This time, however, the terrifying man was even more angry and determined, and Artie no longer had the comfort of his friend by his side.

WHAPPAT!!!!

Before he knew what had happened, Artie was flying through the air. With a *kersplash* he landed in freezing cold water. Turning back he saw that Mary had whipped the frame of his bicycle and yanked it out from under him.

Artie realised that he seemed to be in a fast-flowing current. *The river! He was in the shallows of the river!* The terrible tattooed man dismounted and lumbered towards him in the moonlight, smirking and twirling his whip.

'C'mon, out you get. You don't want to catch a cold now, do you? Come on, boy. You're coming with me …'

WHAPPAT!!!!

Artie felt a searing pain in his leg as Mary's whip caught

hold of him and snaked its way around his calf. Funnel-web and Mr Budgie arrived out of the dark marsh. Puffing and enraged, they started plodding through the mud towards him. Quick as a fish, Artie spun around and dived into the water, jerking on the whip as he went. Mary, holding tight to the other end, went flying face-first into the icy sludge. Cursing and screaming, he flailed about as his motorcycle boots were sucked into the mud. 'GET ME OUT, YOU MORONS! I'M STUCK! HELP ME, YOU NINCOMPOOPS!!!'

Drifting away in the current, Artie watched as the ungainly crew splodged about in the shallows, dragging Mary back to shore.

'I'LL GET YOU, BOY!' the tattooed man bellowed across the water. 'DON'T YOU WORRY! SOONER OR LATER, I'LL GET YOU!!!'

But Artie breathed deep and began stroking out into the darkness of the river. He knew it looped all the way back through the town.

He rolled onto his back, letting the current carry him away, and tried to calm his thoughts.

Bumshoe, was all he could think. *I have to save Bumshoe!*

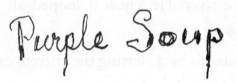

Chapter 13

Purple Soup

Artie stared at the feast laid out in front of him. Hot bread rolls, eggs, sweet tea, a strange purple soup, and, of course, Zoran's nappy cheese.

By the time Artie had drifted back to the centre of town in the icy water, hauled himself out and trudged home, it was dawn. He knew his mum and sister probably wouldn't have noticed his absence. Realising there was no way he could turn up at home now – filthy, soaking wet and having not slept all night – Artie had continued on to the Unpronounceable-enkos, where within minutes he had been ushered inside by Oksana and into a deep, hot bath. She had told him to leave his filthy clothes outside the bathroom door, and had thrown them in to wash while Zoran laid out a mountain of food for breakfast, which Artie now sat in front of, swaddled in Zoran's gigantic dressing-gown.

The little Unpronounceable-enko twin sisters giggled at this vision, but the rest of the family, including Gladys, looked very troubled.

'Artie, what happened?' she said.

'Let him eat, Gladys,' chided Zoran, who was sitting forward, staring wide-eyed at Artie and clearly desperate for answers himself. 'Here,' he said, gently pushing a giant bowl of soup towards Artie. 'Eat this. It's my borsch. I make from beetroot. Yummy!'

Artie stared momentarily at the substance, which was so purple it looked as if it would glow in the dark.

Being too polite to say no, however, Artie lifted a spoonful of the stuff to his mouth.

'Mmm...it looks really...nice,' he said, prepared for the worst. Incredibly, though, it actually tasted *delicious*! It was so bizarre, he almost could have invented it himself!

In spite of the pleasant surprise of Zoran's purple soup, Artie had no appetite. He was too worried about Bumshoe.

He wanted to tell the Unpronounceable-enkos what had happened, but his head was full of thoughts, swirling around like leaves in a storm. If only he'd gone to get the camera by himself. It was all his fault! He was faster ... smaller. He wouldn't have goofed about like Bumshoe. Everything would have been alright. But instead, Bumshoe was now captive to a gang of horrendous thieves, awaiting an unknown fate!

'Artie, what happened?' enquired Oksana gently.

'Let him eat, Oksana,' said Zoran, who was trying to stay calm, but was so desperate to know what had happened that he could barely sit in his seat. Artie tried to spoon another mouthful of purple soup, but his hand didn't seem able to do it.

Unable to bear the suspense any longer, Zoran finally leapt up and bellowed, 'Artie! What happened?'

Artie took a deep breath. 'Well ... there is this cave,' he

began. 'And a robber with a tattoo on his face with spelling mistakes and a man with a birdcage on his head – that's Mr Budgie. And there's also Funnel-web, and Tinkerbell ...'

Artie saw Zoran and Oksana exchange a worried glance. He went on.

'They're the ones who are stealing everything. They stole Gareth the tortoise.'

Gladys took a sharp breath.

'We filmed them, but then Bumshoe got trapped in Mary's sidecar and fell down in a washing machine and they caught him.'

Artie heard himself speaking and suddenly realised how ridiculous the whole thing sounded. But in spite of this, the sheer relief he felt at telling the whole story made him unable to stop.

'I escaped out the window hanging on to Funnel-web's braces. But that gave him a wedgie. And then Tinkerbell bit him on the bum and I floated home.'

The twins were now giggling uncontrollably. Zoran looked sadly at Oksana and gave a little head-shake.

'Shush, girls!' he cried. 'Artie ... This story ...'

'It's not a story,' Artie said. 'It's what happened!'

'Artie,' said Oksana, smiling gently. 'It's a wonderful thing to have a big imagination. And we know that things can be ... a little difficult for you at home. You must miss your dad ...'

'I'm not making it up,' protested Artie. 'They've caught Bumshoe! And they've got Gareth!'

Oksana took Artie's hand across the table and stroked it gently. 'It's alright, Artie. If ever you need help, we are here for you.'

Artie knew it was no use. He couldn't blame the Unpronounceable-enkos for not believing him. He was the boy who cried wolf ... Only this time he was crying Mary, Funnel-web, Mr Budgie and Tinkerbell! It sounded completely nuts. If it weren't for the awful fact that Bumshoe was now their prisoner, he wouldn't believe it himself!

His clothes still warm from the dryer, Artie thanked Zoran and Oksana, and clutching the bag of sandwiches and a library book that she insisted he take, he closed the front door and dejectedly set off for school. The door flew open immediately behind him. It was Gladys.

'Artie!' she whispered. 'I believe you.'

He spun around to look at her, and felt his face flush as purple as Zoran's beetroot soup.

'Thanks,' he murmured.

'Do you think you can save Bumshoe and Gareth?'

'Yes,' said Artie. 'I'll save them.' He turned and set off once more. But the fact of the matter was that Artie had no clue how to save them. He was in completely unknown territory. Once again he thought of his dad's words about how the best discoveries happen when you step into the unknown. But Artie just couldn't figure how that could be, in a situation as tangled and dangerous as this. *Maybe*, he thought bitterly, *it only applied to people who were already strong and brave: to tightrope walkers, or trapeze artists!* Artie trudged onwards to school, his heart full of dread.

Chapter 14

Star Jumps

Why was grammar even invented? This was the question that was ringing in Artie's head as he sat in class listening to Mrs Meller. Well, he wasn't really listening to Mrs Meller at all, he was only *hearing* her.

Mrs Meller was mostly referred to by the students as Mrs Smeller. Bumshoe maintained that you could call her that to her face without her even noticing.

Mrs Meller made Mr Graystains seem like the most vivacious and exciting teacher on earth, *(even though, as we've already discussed, dear reader, Mr Graystains was the most boring teacher in the galaxy.)*

Mrs Meller had a mouth like a drawstring purse, which, when angry, would snap into a hard little knot, but when talking about her favourite things, like conjunctions and prepositions, it would flap open and closed with dreary enthusiasm.

Mrs Meller had a particular dislike of Artie. She liked things to be ordered, clean and neat, and Artie, of course, was none of those things. He was never prepared for his lessons, and he often skipped a shower or two because, well ... because he could.

One of Mrs Meller's favourite tricks was to use Artie as an example to illustrate points of grammar. She would write sentences on the whiteboard like:

The boy was lazy, grubby and unpunctual.

The messy boy has holes in his socks.

If the boy doesn't bathe, nobody will want to sit next to him.

Artie sat in her class daydreaming, and was remembering one particular time when she had said, 'The small boy needs to have a shower ... What is the subject of that sentence, class?'

Nate's hand had shot straight up in the air.

'Yes, Mr Grime?'

'The subject is *Artie*, Mrs Meller.' Some snickers erupted around the class, and Wart doubled over, shaking with silent laughter.

'Er...um...well,' said Mrs Meller, attempting to conceal a little smirk. 'That's not quite what I meant ...'

'But it is, Mrs Smeller!' came Bumshoe's voice. The whole

class turned. Bumshoe continued, 'The subject *is* really Artie, because you like to embarrass him, Mrs Smeller.'

'How DARE you!' snapped the teacher. 'The subject of the sentence is *"the boy".*'

'Yeah, but you really mean Artie, to try and make him feel bad, because you enjoy that.' Bumshoe shrugged matter-of-factly. The class fell utterly silent. Even Wart stopped giggling and stared, slack-mouthed, between the teacher and Bumshoe. Mrs Meller's mouth sprang into a knot that was so tight it looked as if the circulation had been cut off altogether and she may actually end up with gangrene of the lip. And Bumshoe received lunchtime detention for the following two weeks.

Artie felt terrible. He gazed now at the empty seat where Bumshoe normally sat. His friend had done that for him, got himself into trouble, to try to help him. And Artie had repaid him by leaving him alone in the hands of the world's freakiest gang of robbers! Who knew where Bumshoe was at this moment, or what was befalling him? An awful wave of panic overtook him.

His heart pounding like a jackhammer, he suddenly noticed that Mrs Meller seemed to be pointing at the board but talking directly at him!

'… look at this centre clause. Is the shorter clause next to it a relative clause or not?'

The whole class turned to stare at Artie.

'Have you been listening to me, Mr Small?' she hissed.

'Yes, Mrs Meller.'

'Then what did I just say?'

'Um … You said, "Look at Santa Claus. Is the shorter Claus a relative of Santa Claus, or not?"'

Laughter exploded across the room like a volcano.

Artie looked about wildly. On the other side of the room

he could see Gladys, who, far from laughing, was looking extremely worried.

He could no longer contain his panic. His breath was coming in little gasps and his heart was thumping so hard that he couldn't sit still.

He leapt up and, staring at Mrs Meller, began bouncing on the spot, doing star jumps.

The class was now convulsed with laughter. The star jumps became bigger and bigger, until finally Artie was springing all over the room like a mad kangaroo.

'SIT DOWN AT ONCE, MR SMALL!' bellowed Mrs Meller. 'SIT DOWN, I TELL YOU! IT'S A RED CARD FOR YOU! A RED CARD, I TELL YOU!'

But Artie couldn't control his limbs. Try as he might he could not stop leaping about, his arms flailing up and down. Gladys was suddenly beside him, trying to hold him still.

'Artie! Artie! It's alright … calm down …'

Mrs Meller continued her shrieking.

'RED CARD! AUTOMATIC EXPULSION! RED CARD!'

Before he knew it, Artie had bounced out of the classroom and down the corridor. SPROING. SPROING. SPROING.

Then he was running as fast as he could through the school gates and off into the town. At last, he slowed and caught his breath. Star jumps? Really? Why was he doing star jumps? In a grammar lesson? In front of Gladys! The whole class must have thought he was completely mental! And maybe he *was* mental … Maybe all the worry about Bumshoe had made him lose his mind!

He could never go back to school, that was certain. He would go and live in a hollow tree somewhere in a forest, and gather berries and fish for trout. (First of all he was going to have to learn to like trout ...) He would become a hermit. There would be no stepping into the unknown. No gangs with filed teeth and tattooed faces, or star jumps out of grammar class! Just his hollow tree, and his berries and trout.

Before long, Artie began to realise that he was heading in the direction of the robbers' factory. His mind was racing faster than his feet.

Somehow ... somehow, he had to save his friend!

Chapter 15

The FARTEX 120Y

As he neared Aunty-boy's house, he heard it rocking on its foundations as she thundered away at the piano. He snuck past, trying to avoid being spotted. He had no time to lose.

But sure enough, just as he was creeping by, the piano stopped, the window flew open and Aunty-boy stuck her head out.

'Cup of cocoa, coco-loco?' she cooed, clacking her dentures out at him. Macaroni the dog joined her at the window, and gave Artie an excited woof.

Not wanting to seem rude, Artie said, 'Okay, thanks, Aunty-boy.' He dutifully waited at her door as he heard all the locks and bolts being flung open.

'Quick-sticks!' she cried, bobbing from one foot to another in a little dance. 'In you pop. Hoppity-hop!' She slammed the door behind him and set about re-locking it.

Artie had never been inside Aunty-boy's home. It was very dark, and he was amazed at how soft the carpet felt under his feet, until he realised that what he was standing on was a thick layer of baby powder! Every surface in the entire house was coated with the repulsive stuff. It looked like the inside of a snow dome. As Artie shuffled down the corridor, a cloud puffed up, covering him from head to toe.

Aunty-boy set a cup of watery cocoa in front of him, with little islands of white talc floating on top of it.

'Why aren't you in school, custard pie?' she cried.

Artie hesitated. There was no point trying to tell anyone what had happened. It all sounded too nutty! Then again, if anyone was going to believe such a nutty story, it would most likely be someone who actually *was* nuts!

'Well … This is why I'm not in school,' he began. And before he knew it he had recounted his entire story from beginning to end, all the way from Nate throwing his shoes over the telephone lines, through Bumshoe's capture, to star-jumping out of school.

To Artie's amazement, Aunty-boy was very good at listening. She sat bobbing her head from side to side and clucking at all the scary bits. At the end of Artie's story she sat blinking at him through her goggle lenses and saying, 'Poop! Poop! Poop!'

Artie felt quite relieved.

'Off to the police we go!' she cried.

'We can't go to the police!' exclaimed Artie.

'Why not, gooseberry tart?'

'Well, because … because …'

Artie knew exactly why. If he turned up alone at the police station and tried to tell his outlandish story it would be bad enough. But if he arrived with Aunty-boy as well, they'd probably just ship them both straight off to a mental care facility!

'I can't talk to the police about it,' continued Artie. 'I need to go back to the robbers' factory myself and somehow get Bumshoe out!'

'I'm coming too, cream puff!' she chirped. 'We'll need energy!' she added, thrusting a packet of biscuits at him. Artie stared at them for a second. They had obviously been opened about ten years prior, were crawling with weevils, and had a generous coating of baby powder.

'Quick. Straight down the biscuit-hole!' said Aunty-boy, shaking them at him and glaring through her spectacles.

Unable to say no, Artie took one of the revolting objects

and, shaking away as many weevils as he could, chewed off a little chunk. Aunty-boy took a great chomp from hers and sat munching merrily in front of him, her eyes closed in utter pleasure.

Feeling the weevils scuttling around inside his mouth, Artie realised he was never going to be able to swallow the horrible mass.

'Excushe me ... um ... I need to ushe the baffroom, pleashe?'

'Down the corridor on the left, sausage pie!' Aunty-boy exclaimed, helping herself to another weevil and powder treat.

Artie bolted down the hall. Slamming the bathroom door behind him, he spat the hideous wriggling mouthful into the toilet and, along with the rest of the biscuit, flushed it away.

As he was returning along the corridor, Artie noticed a door that was slightly ajar. Through the gap he could see all kinds of equipment, and couldn't help but push the door open a little more. The room was a proper *laboratory*! There were chemicals of all colours in glass beakers, bubbling away and emitting strange smells. There were odd bits and pieces of machinery and metal parts everywhere. On a long table in the middle of the room sat all manner of incredible mechanical objects.

'Haha!'

Artie jumped out of his skin. It was Aunty-boy, right behind him.

'You've spotted my toys!' she exclaimed excitedly. 'My toys, my toys, my pride, my joys!'

'What ... are they exactly?' whispered Artie.

'I'm ready for the showdown, toffee-cake!' said Aunty-boy.

'What showdown?' said Artie.

'When the aliens invade from the planet Zuthor!' she whispered. 'I've been listening to their conversations on my radio. I know what they're up to! And I'm ready!' she cried. With this she gave a little whoop and a jig.

Artie couldn't tell whether she was joking or not. 'Did you make all these yourself?' he asked in amazement.

'Of course, of course, chocolate sauce!'

She stroked an object that looked like an intricate collection of intertwined pipes, gazing at it fondly. 'The Fartex 120Y. A launcher that fires capsules of hydrogen sulphide, otherwise known as rotten-egg gas!'

'And this ...' She smiled, picking up a black shiny ball about the size of a grapefruit, with a red pin sticking out of it. 'My treasure! The Prickle-ator ... Once the pin is pulled, after ten seconds she sends out thousands of needles! POOF!'

'Cool!' breathed Artie. He was beginning to see Aunty-boy in a whole new light. 'What about this?' he asked, lifting a heavy, two-handled machine attached to a large canister. Some thick yellow goo oozed out the end of it.

'Ahhhh! Take care. Take care. My beauty! The Super-Snotter! She fires marvellous streams of synthetic snot up to fifty metres.' And with a note of slight disappointment she added, 'I'm trying to extend its range.'

Artie couldn't believe his eyes. He was sure that none of the weapons actually worked, but still, they were amazing-looking objects ... Maybe Aunty-boy wasn't so nuts after all!

'And what's this?' said Artie, wide-eyed, pointing at something that looked exactly like a cheese sandwich. 'It looks *exactly* like a cheese sandwich!'

A Cheese Sandwich

'It is a cheese sandwich,' said Aunty-boy, offering no further explanation. Artie noticed a silver necklace lying at the very end of the table. Carefully picking it up, he gazed at the little pendant attached to it. It was a tiny figurine of two trapeze artists, one suspended from the other's arms. They swung gently on the heavy chain.

'Hmmm … that's a lucky charm, carrot cake.'

'It's beautiful,' murmured Artie.

'Do you know who gave me that?'

'No,' said Artie.

'Your dad! As a thank-you gift for teaching him the piano.'

Artie was gobsmacked! He knew his dad had played the piano. One of his famous stunts was playing a sonata on a toy piano upside down on the flying trapeze. But he'd had no idea that his dad had learned from Aunty-boy.

'Pop it on. And don't ever take it off, cinnamon buns!

When the aliens arrive from Zuthor, you'll be needing all the luck you can get. And a Fartex 120Y!' she said, blinking at him through her thick lenses.

Artie stared at the trinket. He was awe-struck to think that his dad had touched this very object, and had chosen it for Aunty-boy as a special present. Beaming, Artie fastened it around his neck.

'Quick! Let's bounce, beachball! No time to dilly-dally! Off to the robbers' den!' Aunty-boy chirped.

Macaroni woofed and bounded ahead of them to the front door.

Unlatching all the locks, Aunty-boy threw the door open. There, standing on the porch, were Nate and Wart.

Chapter 16

'We wanna word with you, Farty Artie,' said Nate, his tiny eyes glittering.

'Hehehe,' chuckled Wart, who was hovering behind him, chewing on a raw onion. 'You said "Farty".'

'Shut up, Wart!' hissed Nate.

PLAAACK! Aunty-boy clacked her dentures out at the two boys. 'Off you go, butterscotches!' she exclaimed. Macaroni began barking wildly.

'We're not talking to you, you crazy old biddy!' Nate growled.

'Don't speak to her like that … please,' said Artie quietly.

'Oh yeah?' grinned Nate. 'What are you going to do about it, Farty?'

'Hehehe … "Farty". Again!' snickered Wart.

'SHUT UP, Wart!'

Nate suddenly shoved Aunty-boy with all his might. The poor woman fell backwards into the doorway, as Nate slammed it shut on both her and her dog. Meanwhile Wart grabbed hold of Artie, lifted him up, and hung him by the collar from a coat-rack on the porch wall. He then moved swiftly to the door and put all his weight against it to stop Aunty-boy from coming back out. Behind the door Macaroni was still barking wildly.

Nate swaggered over to where Artie dangled, his feet kicking helplessly in midair.

'So, Farty ...' Nate began.

'Hehehe,' chuckled Wart again, but Nate spun around and glared at him. Wart gulped and fell silent.

'Why did you go loony in Smeller's class and run away?' Nate continued. 'Got something on your mind, have you?'

'No,' whispered Artie.

'Well,' he snarled. 'Your fat friend Bumshoe has been trespassing at my dad's work. My dad's *the mayor*! Do you know what that means? It means he knows everything that's going on. They caught your chubby friend, but it's caused my dad a whole lot of trouble. According to reports, there was a skinny boy with him who escaped. Now seeing as you two are such good pals, I put two and two together, and guess what I came up with?'

'Four?' offered Wart.

'No, not four, you meathead!' snapped Nate. 'I came up with *Artie.*'

Wart looked baffled. 'But two plus two equals …'

'WILL YOU SHUT UP, WART!'

Wart retreated into a bewildered silence, leaning against the door and chomping on the remainder of his onion. On the other side of the door Macaroni continued to bark furiously.

'So my dad and the nice men who work for him are very keen to meet you,' Nate continued. 'That's lucky, isn't it? Because we've just been listening in on your conversation with crazy old Aunty-mental, and you two were on your way to the factory. So why don't I escort you down there, and I can introduce you?'

Before he knew it, Artie was shoved onto the crossbar of Wart's bicycle. Wart clamped his hefty arms on either side of him and pushed off, dinking him down the hill to his doom.

After all that raw onion, Wart began letting out a series of huge burps, and because he was leaning forward, Artie copped the full brunt of each stinking onion puff! Artie actually found himself wishing they'd hurry up and arrive at his doom so he didn't have to inhale any more of that stench. He thought about Aunty-boy, and felt sick at the idea that she might have been hurt when Nate shoved her.

'You're gonna regret sticky-beaking around my dad's work and causing him so much trouble...' Nate called as he pulled alongside them on his incredibly expensive-looking bike. 'My dad's *the mayor*, you know! Nobody messes with my dad!'

'Yeah!' said Wart. 'Nobody messes with Nate's dad. His dad's *the mayor*, you know!'

'I just said that!' snapped Nate.

'Yeah, I know …' said Wart.

'Shut up, Wart!!!'

'Okay, Nate.'

Artie couldn't believe it. Here he was, being dinked to his doom, having to listen to the dumbest conversation in history, and being burped all over by someone called Wart. Could things get any worse?

He was pondering this turn of events when a dark flash of fur came flying through the air. It was Macaroni! He leapt up and snapped at Nate's heels. Nate's bike wobbled crazily and, screaming, he flew straight over the handlebars. Macaroni, meanwhile, circled back, jumped up and sank his fangs into Wart's hefty thigh.

'AAAAAARRRRRRGHHHH,'

came the horrible oniony shriek, as the huge boy lost control.

Artie found himself bouncing softly into a pile of leaves by the roadside. Wart, however, landed with a thump on top of Nate, where he lay bellowing in pain.

'Get off me, you big ape!' yelled Nate, smacking Wart in the ribs.

'I've been bit! I've been bit!' cried Wart, clutching at his wound.

'I DON'T CARE!' screamed Nate. 'GET OFF ME!'

Macaroni raced about, snarling and snapping at the two of them as they crawled from the wreckage of their mangled bikes.

'STATUE!!!' came a familiar voice from right beside Artie. Macaroni immediately froze as still as a ... well, as still as a statue. Artie looked up. There next to him, bobbing around and humming a little ditty, was Aunty-boy. Supporting her bicycle with one hand, she held out an open packet to Artie with the other, and gave it a shake.

'Bickie?' she chirped, and clacked out her falsies.

Chapter 17

Artie soon found himself in an even less comfortable position than the cross-bar of Wart's bicycle: squished down into the front shopping basket of Aunty-boy's bike.

She was a truly dreadful rider. At every stop sign she began to speed up, whistling and humming as she careened between swerving cars. She veered all over the road, completely ignoring the painted lines. She sailed straight through red traffic lights, bringing cars to a screeching halt, and leaving a trail of near-accidents. If anyone beeped their horns at her or yelled things she would give them a little wave and a smile and then poke her dentures out at them.

But despite the terrifying ride, his discomfort squashed up in the basket, and the fact that they were heading into a potentially horrifying situation at the factory, Artie felt surprisingly content. He was no longer alone on his adventure, and seeing all of Aunty-boy's inventions had given him a new respect for her. Then of course there was their secret weapon, loping along joyfully beside them: Macaroni!

BLAT!

For the first time since the whole awful encounter with Mayor Grime's gang, Artie allowed himself to imagine that things might actually turn out alright. Maybe they'd arrive at the factory and Macaroni would round up the whole gang, who would then simply hand over Bumshoe and give themselves up. He could rescue Gladys's tortoise and hand him back to her personally. Everything would be well in the world again!

It was starting to get dark when they arrived at the factory. Immediately, it became clear that something was very, very wrong …

The place was deserted. There were no security guards and the gates hung open. Apart from scattered rubbish, empty boxes and a few other signs of hasty departure, the factory itself was completely *abandoned*. A few feeble lights flickered on and off. There was no trace of the robbers' gang in sight.

'But they were here …' said Artie, bewildered, as he wandered through the vast, echoing space. 'I promise! They were right here. The place was full of stuff … Here's where they were painting cars!' he cried, pointing at an empty corner of the building. 'And see! See that window? That was where I ran up all the musical instruments and bungee-jumped down using Funnel-web's braces!'

'Of course, of course, buttermilk pancake ...' said Aunty-boy, blinking at him through her glasses. 'But there's nothing we can do about it now, so it's time to head home for some sweeties, a nice cup of cocoa, a little shower of baby powder, and off to bed! Care to join me for din-dins?'

Artie looked at her sadly.

'No. Thanks, Aunty-boy. I'll be alright. I can walk home.'

'Toodle-pip, then,' said Aunty-boy, and she mounted her squeaky old bike and wobbled out of the factory, Macaroni trotting along behind.

Artie had never felt so alone in his life. Alone and confused. What could have happened to Bumshoe? How could he get *anyone* to believe him now?

He had no sooner turned to begin the long trudge home, when dark figures began pouring in through the doors. Funnel-web, Mr Budgie, and the workers from the factory were arriving from all sides. Nate and Wart were there too, battered and bruised from their recent encounter. Nate leered at Artie as he approached, holding up a mobile phone.

'Have you heard of these?' he snarled. 'They're called *mobile phones*. It's how most of the world stays in contact. So I can call my dad and his friends and tell them that you're on your way!

Oh … but maybe you haven't heard of them because you're so
poor!'

'Yeah,' Wart chimed in. 'Maybe you haven't heard of them
because you're so poor!'

'That's *what I just said*!' snarled Nate, under his breath.

'Yeah, I know, Nate,' whispered Wart. 'I was just lending
you support. You know, kind of repeating it for effect …'

'I don't need your support! Think of your own things to
say!'

'It really hurts my feelings when you say things like that,'
Wart sniffed. 'I'm only ever trying to help. Just because we're
bad doesn't mean we have to be *nasty*.'

'Yes it does! That's exactly what
it means, you gumby!!!' bellowed Nate.

Artie stared at his shoes. For the second time that day
he was being subjected to a very tedious argument between
the two bullies. He didn't really know what to do while they
bickered among themselves.

'Boys, boys, calm down,' croaked Funnel-web, stepping
towards Artie. 'We've got important work to do!'

There was a sudden earth-shattering blast as **MARY** burst through the main doors of the factory on his motorbike.

Artie was trapped. Completely, utterly, horribly, inescapably *trapped*.

Chapter 18

Grime House

Funnel-web and Mary were scary from a distance, but up close they were really, **really, really** scary. Mary's ginormous bike growled to a stop centimetres from Artie's toes, and he dismounted. Both men came right up close to Artie's face and stared. Mary was smiling, but it wasn't a nice smile, like the smile that Gladys gave him sometimes when she called out 'Hello' on the way to school, or the type that Bumshoe gave him when he rattled an open bag of Chococaramel-Cococreambombs at him, or the kind that his mum used to give him back in the Jurassic days when she'd ask if he'd like some mango with his breakfast. It was an awful and sinister smile, which, combined with his tattooed head, made Artie's blood turn to ice.

Funnel-web, however, was not smiling at all.

'You stretched my braces beyond repair,' he breathed,

displaying the two long straps flapping uselessly by his sides. 'And look at this!' he cried, turning around and lifting the back of his filthy shirt. A huge red wound ran right up the middle of his back.

'That's from your wedgie! It looks like my bottom starts up at my neck. IT'S VERY EMBARRASSING!!' he bellowed.

'Sorry,' Artie murmured. 'Um … can you tell me where my friend is?'

'Oh! Oh! It's all about your *friend*, is it?' sneered the spidery face. 'No concern at all for my *braces* and giving me a *wedgie*, and causing me to have an *embarrassing bottom*???'

'Would you like to see your friend?' interjected Mary.

'Yes…' replied Artie timidly. Was Bumshoe still here at the factory somewhere? Maybe the gang was going to let him go … perhaps with a warning to stay away! Artie allowed himself a glimmer of hope.

'Please, I'd really like to see him,' he said.

Mary and Funnel-web glanced at one another.

'He'd like to visit his friend,' said Mary.

'Well, I suppose that's only fair …' said Funnel-web.

'Quite so. Shall we take him for a visit?' said Mary, whose smile was dissolving into a snicker.

'Of course. We can all have a lovely dinner together.' At this Funnel-web burst into laughter. Soon everyone was rocking backwards and forwards and cackling. Artie suddenly found himself missing his mum. Even though he knew at that moment she would probably just be lying in bed staring at the wall or watching the telly, he wished more than anything in the world that he was snuggling up next to her ...

But within minutes, he found himself in a car driven by Funnel-web, sandwiched in the back between Nate and Wart. Funnel-web, having captured Artie, now seemed very cheerful and kept turning around to the boy and baring his sharpened fangs in a horrific smile.

Behind them, Artie could hear the rhythmic thudding of Mary's motorbike. They drove through the dark streets, and began winding up the hills into the fancy part of town. The higher they climbed, the bigger the houses became, until finally Artie couldn't see any houses at all because they were hidden among grand gardens behind massive walls.

Eventually they arrived at a humungous gate, manned by security guards, which immediately swung open, allowing them to sweep inside. They drove up an inky gravel driveway

which seemed to go on forever until, finally, they arrived at the biggest house that Artie had ever seen.

'Welcome to Grime House,' breathed Funnel-web.

The car crunched to a stop and Artie was marched inside. Behind the enormous doors, the house was full of gold, marble and shiny, mirrored surfaces.

Some truly awful artworks circled the grand entrance foyer. These included:

1. A gigantic portrait of Nate as a ninja warrior flying through clouds on a winged horse, wielding a battle axe.
2. A golden statue of an enormous muscle-woman, spinning the planet earth on her index finger as if it was a basketball.
3. A sculpture of Mayor Grime as Moses in a toga, reading out the Ten Commandments from a stone tablet.

Dumbfounded, Artie was led past walls of caged animals, which he had no doubt were once family pets like Gareth the tortoise. The poor beasts mewed, croaked, yapped and honked as he passed.

From somewhere in the mansion there came a very odd and unpleasant cooking smell. In all his time preparing elaborate culinary creations Artie had cooked up some pretty stinky dishes, but nothing that stunk as strangely as whatever this smell was …

Funnel-web and Mary dragged Artie by the wrist all the way down a long hallway. They passed what seemed like hundreds of closed doors and ancient portraits of people with tiny little eyes, who were obviously the Grime family ancestors.

The boy's heart was pounding furiously. He hoped he wasn't about to have another attack of star jumps. Where were they taking him? What would he be subjected to next? His mind was galloping, trying to figure out a plan of action or escape, but nothing came to him.

At the end of the hallway, Funnel-web stopped at a tiny door, barely taller than Artie himself.

'Here we are!' exclaimed Mary cheerfully, reaching for a set of keys inside his pocket. He bent down and, making little grunting noises of exertion, unlocked the door.

'There you go, sir. Welcome to your suite,' smiled Mary. 'If there's anything I can do to assist you during your stay at Grime House, please don't hesitate to contact me or my colleagues. Your comfort is our number-one priority.'

At this he and Funnel-web erupted into cackles. Funnel-web gave Artie a shove and the boy clanged down some metal stairs into a dingy cellar, with the robbers following him. A single light bulb illuminated the gloom. There in the corner, tied to a chair, was Bumshoe.

'Artie!' he cried. 'I knew you'd come for me!' Artie was overjoyed to see his friend still alive and apparently unhurt. 'Sorry,' Artie whispered. 'Don't know how much use I'm going to be to you ...' 'Shut up, you two!!' growled Funnel-web. 'No talking allowed!' He grabbed a chair and the two men began tying Artie back-to-back with his friend. Artie yelped in pain as the rope cinched his wrists tight to the chair. 'Now,' said Mary, leaning in to him. 'Mayor Grime sends his apologies, but he is currently rather pressed for time. He does ask that you please be patient, as he is trying to devise some special entertainment for you ...'

With that, the pair stomped up the stairs chuckling, then slammed and bolted the little door behind them.

'Thought they'd never go!' exclaimed Bumshoe. 'Now, how are we going to get out of here?!'

'Not a clue,' replied Artie, wriggling his wrists in a futile effort to loosen the ropes.

'Tell you what, I could do with a feed! This lot haven't given me a bite to eat!'

'Bumshoe ...' said Artie, quietly.

'Yeah?'

'I'm sorry I let you get caught. And then I just ran for it ... I didn't know what else to do.'

'Don't be a goober!' exclaimed his friend. 'You weren't going to be much use to me chewed up in chunks by Tinkerbell, which is exactly what would have happened if you'd stuck around! Which reminds me ...' he went on. 'Who calls a boy dog Tinkerbell?'

'I had the same thought!' Artie chuckled. Even though he was tired to his bones and in such a dire situation, it was a huge relief to be reunited with his friend.

'What do you reckon they're up to?' said Bumshoe.

'Well,' said Artie, stifling a yawn. 'Seems to me that they go out at night robbing the town. They take all the booty and hide it at the cave. Then, over time, they move it all to the factory to be altered a bit and have the serial numbers changed, and then they repackage it and sell it again.'

'Why do they bring all the pets up here to Grime House?' asked Bumshoe, also yawning. 'Did you see them all down the corridor?'

'Hmmm,' Artie mused. 'No idea about that. You didn't happen to see Gareth, did you?'

But there was no reply, and Artie realised his friend had fallen asleep. He sat in deep thought, his mind running over all the possibilities, desperately looking for a solution, until he too finally drifted off into an uncomfortable and fitful sleep.

Chapter 19

Cockerdoodle
Cutlet

The boys were awakened the next morning by the sound of the little door being unlocked and clanking open. A silhouette slid through and unfolded to its full height. There, at the top of the stairs, was the unmistakeable form of Mayor Grime.

The Mayor clanged slowly down the staircase

ting
tang
teng
tong
TUNG

… letting each step ring in the air for effect. Following him down were Mary and Funnel-web, who looked very happy with themselves. The two huge men in sunglasses who seemed to accompany Mayor Grime wherever he went also swept through the door and stood at attention, leaving their sunglasses on despite the dimness of the room.

In the little circle of light from the single bulb, Mayor Grime stopped, his face half in shadow. The terrible cooking stench that Artie had smelt the night before suddenly permeated the room, and the boys noticed that the awful man was gnawing on a bone.

'Hello, boys,' he purred. 'Are you aware of how much *trouble* you've caused me?'

'Um. Not really …' mumbled Artie.

'Well. Let me explain,' said the Mayor, licking some grease from his fingers. Artie noticed that his eyes, which were tiny under normal circumstances, had all but disappeared in the shadowy light, giving the eerie impression of talking to a head without any eyes at all. 'Because you two nosy little pests came sniffing around my properties—'

'You mean the cave and the factory?' said Bumshoe.

'Yesss,' said the Mayor. 'I mean *my* cave and *my* factory.'

'Well. It's not really your cave, to be fair. Nail Can Hill is public land,' reasoned Bumshoe. 'Technically you've just appropriated that cave for your own purposes but really—'

'QUIET!' snarled Mary.

'Now you listen to me, fat boy, and you too, skinny boy,' said the Mayor, poking the air with his bone. 'Because of you two I've decided to close down my entire operation: my cave, my factory – everything! I have run seamless operations in many towns for many years, by always staying two steps ahead, and I'm not about to have my cover blown! So we have moved everything to another town and now we have to begin from scratch. And that costs me money. And there is *NOTHING* I hate more than *LOSING MONEY!!!*'

At this point the Mayor took a moment to suck on the foul-smelling bone. He paused dramatically, before a dreadful smile spread over his face. He extracted the bone from his mouth with a loud *pop*.

'Do you know what this is?' he breathed, waggling it right under Artie's nose.

'No, sir.'

'It's a *cutlet of puppy*. "Labradoodle", I believe, or some such ridiculous composite of which the public are so inordinately fond these days.'

'From memory it might have been a "Cavoodle", Mayor,' grinned Funnel-web.

'Or perhaps a "Cockerdoodle"?' said the Mayor, and he, Funnel-web and Mary burst into a fit of mad giggles.

'Do you know, I *only* eat meat, boys?' The Mayor by this time had his face right next to Artie's. His minuscule eyes seemed to be peering directly into the boy's soul. 'Veggies are for *sissies*,' he whispered. 'But *meat* is for *men* … And do you know where all my meat comes from?'

Once again he paused for effect.

'*Pets!*' the Mayor exclaimed happily. He seemed thrilled with the idea, as if it had just occurred to him.

'*Pets!* All kinds! It doesn't matter! They're all delicious! And do you know why?' (Once again the dramatic pause …)

'Because they're so *pampered*! Their flesh is exquisitely

tender and succulent because the dear things are so loved and coddled their whole lives!' The Mayor became increasingly excited. Some gobs of white foam began to appear at the corner of his mouth. 'It's a marvellous system, really. All you townsfolk spend your lives carefully preparing and fattening these superb meaty treats: pussy cats, terrapins, puppy dogs, guinea piggies, bunny rabbits … just for *me*! *The Mayor!* The most important person in the entire town-and-the-immediate-outlying-district. So thoughtful. So kind!'

With this the Mayor began a sort of delirious waltz all by himself. Mary and Funnel-web exchanged a slightly concerned glance. But then both men merely gazed at the Mayor with little indulgent smiles, and began clapping along in time.

He really is completely bonkers, thought Artie.

Suddenly the Mayor stopped and sprang forward right up into Bumshoe's face.

'I've been thinking about you boys, and how you're going to have to REPAY me for all the MONEY you've MADE ME LOSE!!!' As he screamed the little pools of white foam that had gathered in the corners of his mouth atomised and sprayed all over the unfortunate boy's face.

'Aaaaaaaaaaah ...'

howled Bumshoe, straining to wriggle free.

'Oooooh, I'm sorry, did I *scare* you?'

'No, it's not that!' exclaimed Bumshoe. 'It's just ... You completely covered my face with ... whatever that cheesy goo around your mouth is, and it's just ... really ... *gross*!'

The Mayor fixed the boys with a stare, and patted strands of slick hair down to his scalp.

'I've just had a *brainwave*. Do you see, gentle friends?' he said, turning to Mary and Funnel-web. 'This is why I'm the Mayor, the most important person in the entire town-and-the-immediate-outlying-district, and all of you are just ... well ... all of you ...' he giggled.

'Fire up the ovens, gentlemen! I'm about to expand my culinary repertoire! After all, what could be more tender than the meat of boys who have been so gently cared for? Nurtured and loved their entire lives ... Boy kebabs, anyone?'

The Mayor began to giggle again.

Tears sprang to Artie's eyes. *He isn't serious,* he thought. *Surely he's just trying to scare us!*

'Actually, Artie's pretty much raising himself, so he hasn't been gently cared for at all, plus he eats a whole lot of really weird stuff,' cried Bumshoe.

Artie could tell by the tone of his voice that his friend was taking the Mayor's threat seriously.

'You don't wanna go eating him – you'll get *sick*! And as for me – well – I've got about the worst diet in the whole world! Everybody says so. I just eat junk food and Chococaramel-Cococreambombs. I'm only going to taste of refined sugars and preservatives. I'll be terrible for your cholesterol—'

'SHUT UP!' bawled Mary and Funnel-web simultaneously.

'Righto,' sniffed Bumshoe.

Artie heard him stifling a sob.

The Mayor bounced up the stairs, elated at the brilliance of his own plan.

ting

tang

teng

tong

TUNG

'*Quick*, boys, *quick*!' he called down to the two robbers. 'I've worked up a terrible appetite!' He paused for a moment at the top of the stairs as one of the huge men in sunglasses unlocked the little door. 'And gentlemen,' he said, 'I think perhaps *rosemary* or *thyme* with boy-meat, don't you?'

'Oh, yes, very much so,' nodded Funnel-web.

'Indeed,' said Mary.

'*Exciting!*' the Mayor cried, clasping his hands together in the shadows. 'New culinary horizons, boys!'

And with that he slid out of the room, the men in sunglasses on his heels, slamming the door behind them.

Chapter 20

The Statue

The terrified boys were dragged by Mary and Funnel-web back down the long hallway towards the grand entrance foyer. Up ahead they could hear the noises of all the animals in cages. The boys were still tied back-to-back, and had to shuffle in an awkward crab-like way.

Artie gazed miserably up at the passing parade of Grime family ancestors with their hard little eyes. He longed to be able to see his friend's face. *Bumshoe will have an idea any second,* he thought. *Bumshoe always has ideas!*

Artie listened in growing distress as the two robbers planned the boys' grisly fate.

'Right ... We'll clean and gut them out the back of the kitchen where we do all the bigger pets,' said Mary. 'Then I'll do the butchering because you're not much chop with that, pardon the pun,' he chuckled.

'Yeah, alright, alright,' replied Funnel-web, who sounded slightly wounded.

'Sorry, didn't mean to be rude,' explained Mary. 'I just think you're much better with the smaller animals. I mean, you did a terrific job with those hamsters, for instance.'

'Do you think so?' replied Funnel-web.

'Absolutely first rate, my friend!' said Mary. 'Now, I'm thinking I might do a nice French-trimmed rib roast.'

'Ooh, ooh. Lovely ...' said Funnel-web. 'Just lovely.'

'And I know the boss suggested rosemary or thyme, but I'm really thinking *sage* will be the go.'

'Awwww – bit risky, don't you think?' Funnel-web said with a fretful note.

'Trust me. Once he tastes it, he'll love it. It was the same with kittens and oregano.'

They began passing the rows of caged animals and Artie realised they were nearing the grand entrance. He half-heartedly glanced around to see if he could spot Gareth, but knew that he was hardly in any position now to rescue the animal.

'Now, I'm going to have a lot of work to do on the chubby one to trim off all that lard,' continued Mary, 'and I'm concerned the skinny one won't have any beautiful marbling on the meat.'

The boys were dragged through the ghastly sculptures and paintings that ringed the foyer. The two robbers came to an abrupt halt.

'What the blue blazes is *that*?' cried Mary.

Artie craned his head to see what they were looking at but the men blocked his view.

'When did this thing arrive?' the tattooed man asked.

'No idea,' said Funnel-web.

'The boss must have organised it. Or more likely Mrs Grime,' whispered Mary. 'Yes, it's definitely more Mrs Grime's aesthetic.'

There was a moment of silence.

'It's a terribly ugly work,' he continued, thoughtfully. 'I mean, it has none of the neo-classical charm that it so stridently aims for.'

'I'm afraid I don't agree,' said Funnel-web. 'It's perhaps a tad *confused*. But the artist's sense of line and the composition of the forms is very powerful, don't you find? One can't remain unmoved by it …'

'Not in the least,' argued Mary with a headshake. 'It has pretensions far beyond its limitations. On the one hand it beckons the classical and on the other it's striving for the post-modern, and failing in all quarters …'

'Well,' said Funnel-web, tersely. 'To be fair, when it comes to art, I've probably got a bit more of a clue …'

'What's *that* supposed to mean?' snapped Mary.

'I was the one who studied art!'

'Just because you studied it doesn't mean you *understand* it!' growled the huge man.

'I had a very promising career as an artist, I'll have you know!' said Funnel-web.

'Until your promising career as a house burglar got in the way!' said Mary.

Artie didn't care what the two thieves were squabbling over (he frankly couldn't believe that any artwork could be uglier than the portrait of Nate on a winged horse, or Mayor Grime as Moses reading out the Ten Commandments, which he was currently looking at). The awful, inevitable fact began to dawn on him that he and his friend were about to become lunch for a lunatic local politician! His heart rattled like a machine-gun, and he gulped for air.

'You wouldn't know *art* if it jumped up and bit you!' said Mary.

'Says the man whose face has got spelling mistakes tattooed all over it!' cried Funnel-web.

'Well, I did it in the mirror, didn't I? You try tattooing your face in the mirror!'

'No thanks! I'm happy with it the way it is,' roared Funnel-web.

'With your little sharpened teeth? Is that supposed to be *scary*?' said the big man.

'Scarier than having "Eat, Drink and be *Mary*" scrawled across my head! It's a wonder people don't call you "Mary"!'

'We do ...' murmured Bumshoe.

Artie rolled his eyes. Sometimes his friend just couldn't help opening his mouth when he really ought to keep it closed.

There was a silence.

'You *what?*' rumbled Mary.

'Erm. Nothing,' said Bumshoe.

Funnel-web snickered. 'He said they *do*! They *do* call you Mary. Hahahahahaha ...'

'Shut up, Funnel-web!' growled Mary.

'That's the funniest thing I've ever heard, Humphrey!' screeched Funnel-web.

'Wow,' whispered Bumshoe out of the corner of his mouth. 'Mary's real name is *Humphrey*!'

'Shut up, Funnel-web! Or should I say: Reginald!' Mary/Humphrey cried.

'Wow,' whispered Bumshoe. 'And Funnel-web's real name is Reginald!'*

'You shut up, why don't you?' yelled Funnel-web/Reginald.

* Please note, dear reader, for everyone's comfort and on-going pleasure, the characters of Humphrey and Reginald will hereafter continue to be referred to as Mary and Funnel-web.

The men fell silent for a moment, not looking at each other.

Mary sighed. 'I don't know what came over me. I'm terribly sorry,' he murmured.

'No, no,' replied his hairy friend. 'It was all my fault. I was insensitive.'

'Not at all!' exclaimed Mary.

'Anyway,' said Funnel-web. 'Please don't let's speak like that to one another again. I hate it when we quarrel.'

'Hugs?' offered Mary.

'Hugs!' nodded Funnel-web solemnly. And the two robbers came together and gave each other a little cuddle.

'**Now, come on!**' Mary roared, yanking at the boys' rope. 'Boss'll be getting hungry!'

The boys were hauled off once more, crab-walking behind the men.

Artie was petrified. It was becoming clear that neither boy was going to come up with a magical solution to their plight. But as they swept through the grand foyer and down the opposite hallway, Artie and Bumshoe finally caught a glimpse of the artwork the robbers had been bickering over.

There, right alongside the other sculptures, was a life-sized, perfectly white statue of a squat, almost spherical old lady with a dog curled at her feet. It was so true to life, they could almost have been real figures that had been ... *covered in baby powder!*

Artie was gobsmacked. He tried unsuccessfully to look at his friend. But then he heard Bumshoe let out a tiny 'Yesss!' and knew then that he too must have spotted the indisputable, completely unique and wonderful forms of Aunty-boy and Macaroni!

Chapter 21

SIZE 14 CHEF'S CLEAVER

The kitchen door slammed and Mary clapped his hands together with glee.

'Oh, I do love my cooking! Another day ... another recipe! Now, drag them out here if you please, Funnel-web.' He led the way through the kitchen, out into an enclosed courtyard.

Looking up, Artie saw that covering one entire wall of this area were the pelts of hundreds of varieties of animals, which had obviously met their grisly ends in this very place. He swallowed hard. In the middle of the concrete floor was a drainage grate, which was covered in bits of gizzard and gore. The men set to work untying the boys' ropes.

'Could you please do me a favour, my dear friend, and bring me a chopper from the kitchen?' Mary enquired. 'One of the large ones, probably a size fourteen chef's cleaver?'

'Why, of course!' piped Funnel-web. Artie watched, sickened, as the hairy thief disappeared momentarily behind the door.

'DA-DAAAAH!'

The terrible man sprang back into view, waving a giant meat-axe over his head with a theatrical flourish. Artie was horror-struck. What if they had been wrong? Perhaps what they'd seen was just a sculpture, and Aunty-boy and Macaroni weren't coming to their rescue after all! If they were coming they'd really *better get a move on* because—

'OUCH!'

Artie's thought was cut short as he saw a black metallic ball thwack into Funnel-web's bottom and go clattering onto the kitchen floor.

The skinny man squawked, and dropping the meat-axe on the kitchen counter, he rubbed his bruised rear end. Baffled, he glanced about, and then warily bent down to pick up the shiny little object.

'What is it?' asked Mary.

'Dunno,' murmured his friend, gingerly shaking the thing, and sniffing at it. 'But it seems to be … ticking,' he said, bewildered.

BAM!!!! It exploded in a shower of prickles, completely covering the interior of the kitchen, and Funnel-web in particular.

'AAAAAAAAAAARK!'

he screeched, and started rushing around like an angry hedgehog, bumping into walls and tearing at all the needles.

In the courtyard, Mary was casting about wildly. Artie could tell he had no idea what was going on, or where the threat was coming from. At a loss for how to deal with the unknown foe, he finally took up a ju-jitsu stance – directed at nothing in particular.

At that moment, bounding right through the kitchen and into the courtyard came a furry four-legged missile, leaving a trail of white baby powder in the air. Macaroni! He latched straight on to Mary's nose. The tattooed man began squealing, spinning in circles and trying to prise the dog off. But the trusty pooch clung on for dear life.

Funnel-web, meanwhile, had begun rolling around on the kitchen floor, which only prickled him all the more.

Artie watched enthralled as Aunty-boy emerged through the kitchen, looking like a bizarre little ghost, and carrying some kind of huge holster on her back, still covered in her layer of baby powder. She skipped over the writhing figure on the floor, plucked the meat-axe from the kitchen bench, and strode out towards the boys. She lifted the blade high above her head.

'Aunty-boy! It's us! It's us!! Artie and Bumshoe!!!' screamed the boys, terrified that in all the mayhem she had mistaken them for members of the gang.

'Yes, of course, crab-apple dumplings … of course!' she

chirped, then paused for a second and wildly slashed the meat-axe between them.

'AAAAARGH!!!' yelled the boys.

But Aunty-boy had only been severing their ropes – they were free! Artie and Bumshoe jumped around, laughing and whooping.

'How did you find us here?' Artie asked breathlessly.

The little lady tapped the trapeze pendant on Artie's necklace.

'A lovely memento from your dear daddy, but I also took the liberty of installing a top-of-the-range GPS tracker inside …'

'GET THIS ANIMAL OFF ME!!' bawled Mary, who was still spinning in circles beside them with Macaroni swinging off his nose.

Aunty-boy gave a sharp little whistle and the dog immediately unclamped himself and sat quietly, gazing lovingly up at his owner.

'GET IT AWAY FROM ME! PLEASE. I'LL BE GOOD. I PROMISE!' screamed Mary, who had deep doggy-teeth cuts all over his nose. Curiously, Artie noticed that the word 'MARY' of his tattoo now appeared to read more like 'MERRY'. It seemed Macaroni had inadvertently corrected Mary's spelling mistake!*

Mary, clutching at his nose, galloped back inside Grime House, leaping over his prone and prickle-covered comrade.

'Well! Perhaps it's time we all popped off,' said Aunty-boy.

The three of them, with Macaroni in tow, were escaping through the kitchen when the door into the corridor was suddenly blocked by Mayor Grime and the two gigantic men in sunglasses.

'Well!' said the Mayor quietly. 'What's all *this*?' He began moving towards them, his tiny eyes glistening with menace. 'I'm not happy about *this*,' he hissed. 'I'm not happy at all.'

Immediately, Aunty-boy was pressing something into each of the boys' hands. Artie looked down. It was a clothes peg!

'Hold your breath and block your ears, tartlets!' she whispered. Bewildered as they were, the boys clamped the pegs on their noses. Reaching over her shoulder, the old lady tore something from the holster on her back.

---

* Please note, dear reader, that despite this spelling correction the character of Mary will continue to be referred to as Mary.

BOOOOOOOOOOOOOM!

The room shook as if a volcano had erupted under them. *It was the Fartex 120Y!* The far side of the room was filled with stinking green gas. The two boys exchanged a look of astonishment. *The Fartex actually worked!*

'Oh, yes! That's a very good result,' Aunty-boy cried. 'That seemed to go much better than the early trials,' she added, with a little cough. 'And now we have to move rather quickly, boysenberries!' She took a deep breath, and they bolted for the doorway.

Mr Grime and his henchmen were now collapsing and spluttering in the putrid green fug of the kitchen, clawing at their throats. Artie, Bumshoe and Aunty-boy tore straight past them and out the door.

As he rounded the corner, Bumshoe paused, threw a thigh in the air and made his own noisy contribution to the overpowering stench of the kitchen. He then slammed the door behind him, and they took off down the corridor, cackling with glee.

At last they were able to stop and take in a big breath. Artie heard the kitchen door fly open behind them and the men began to spill out into the hallway. Once again, Aunty-boy plucked out the Fartex 120Y.

'Pegs in place and block your ears!!' she ordered the boys.

BOOOOOOOOOOOOM!

The end of the hallway was engulfed in a rancid plume of gas.

Leaving the Mayor and his henchmen bumbling around in the green haze, they continued running for the front door, with Macaroni dashing ahead. As they neared the entrance foyer, they began to encounter the walls of caged animals.

'We've got to set them free!' cried Artie, tearing the peg from his nose. He began throwing open every cage in sight. Aunty-boy and Bumshoe did the same.

Pandemonium erupted in the hallway. Possums, snakes, budgies, rabbits and dogs were scampering, slithering, flapping, hopping and loping in all directions, with Macaroni herding them towards the exit...

Arriving in the entrance foyer, Artie ploughed his way through the traffic jam of confused animals. At last his hand found the gold handle of the front door. He tore it open and then he, Bumshoe, Aunty-boy and Macaroni rushed outside, followed by a steady stream of escaping beasts.

But Artie stopped.

'You go on ahead. There's something I have to do.'

'What?' said Bumshoe. 'You can't stay *here*!'

'I'll catch up with you,' said Artie.

The nauseating gas, having travelled the length of the hallway, was now pouring out through the front door.

'Come on, Master Small, we'd best away!' piped Aunty-boy. Macaroni yapped in agreement.

'Artie!' cried Bumshoe. 'What's wrong with you? You can't

go back in there – they're all *bonkers*! They'll *eat* you! And it's full of gas – including mine. *You really don't want to go in there!*'

Artie, ignoring his friend's plea, turned to Aunty-boy. 'How will you get out through the front gates?' he asked.

Aunty-boy blinked at him through her thick lenses, tapped the two Prickle-ator balls she had attached to her waistband, then turned around and waggled her Fartex at him.

'Never fear when a Fartex is near!' she chirped.

'Great,' he grinned. 'Now, run! *Just go!* I've got a tortoise to save.'

With that, Artie took a deep breath and leapt in through the front door, straight back into the stench, the chaos and the evil of Grime House.

Chapter 22

Gareth

Artie noticed that the fumes were thicker up high, so he threw himself onto all fours and began to crawl. A swarm of escaping animals moved past him in the opposite direction, like Noah's Ark in reverse.

Through the gas, Artie could faintly see the shape of Mayor Grime being ushered through a door off the hallway by the men in sunglasses.

Artie was determined to find Gareth the tortoise. Still holding his breath, he began rummaging through all the cages and searching among all the animals skittering past. Birds flapped into his face and pooed on him, a litter of excited puppies yapped at him, and a giant lizard of some sort clambered over his back.

Artie had held his breath for as long as he could. He urgently needed air, but dared not inhale the noxious fumes from the Fartex 120Y. The gas made his eyes sting and he felt his energy rapidly running out. Then, in the very last bank of cages, he spotted Gareth the tortoise, right at head height and unable to jump down like all the other animals.

Artie reached in and took hold of the little animal, then clutching him gently under one arm, he slid off down the corridor like a snake, trying to stay under the dense green cloud above him.

Finally the front door of the mansion was in sight. Artie leapt up, Gareth cradled carefully in his hands, and allowed himself one huge breath. Unfortunately, the air was still thick with rotten-egg gas, and Artie began hacking and coughing. He pulled at the door handle. Fresh air blew onto his face and he sucked deep, grateful draughts of it into his lungs. Still doubled over and clutching the tortoise tight to his chest, he sprinted down the stairs … straight into the arms of Mayor Grime.

Chapter 23

PRIME CUTS

The Mayor bent down to stare directly into Artie's eyes. Once again, the boy had the creeping feeling that his soul was being peered into. The two men in sunglasses, as ever, stood blankly to attention behind the Mayor.

'Do you like tortoises?' whispered Grime.

'Yes,' said Artie meekly.

The Mayor clicked his fingers, and one of the henchmen lunged forward, grabbing Artie by the shirt, and lifted him up to the Mayor's eye-height. The Mayor studied Artie closely.

'You must *really* like them to put yourself into so much danger,' the Mayor offered. 'Or is it just *this* tortoise in particular that has a special place in your heart?'

Artie stared into the tiny black holes that were the Mayor's eyes.

'I don't know, sir,' he breathed.

'You don't know or you don't want *me* to know?' said the Mayor.

Artie glanced around the garden, desperately hoping that Aunty-boy and Bumshoe had escaped to safety.

'You see, skinny boy,' the Mayor continued. 'You've now put me in a terrible pickle. You have caused me to shut down my business, ransacked my home and set free my pantry. But do you know what the *worst* thing is that you've done?' The Mayor's voice dropped until it was barely audible, but Artie could feel the gigantic volcano of rage beneath the surface. Once again, white bubbles of spit began forming at the edges of his mouth.

'You humiliated me,' he purred. 'So now I need to find a new, very special punishment, and then we can resume our preparations for lunch. I'm trying to discern what that punishment should be … And you're going to help me, you see? Now, who does the tortoise belong to?'

'Don't know,' gasped Artie, who was by this time almost being strangled by the force of the henchman's hands.

'Dad! Dad! I know whose tortoise it is!' cried a familiar voice.

And there, right beside Artie, was Nate.

'It belongs to the foreigner girl, who lives next door to Farty Artie!' Nate continued. 'She's always going on at school about her stupid pet tortoise and posting pictures of it online! Plus, everyone knows Farty Artie has a crush on her, so it all makes sense!'

Artie felt himself being gradually lowered to the ground by the man in sunglasses. The Mayor gazed down at the boy with a little smile.

'You see, that's why my family is the most important in the entire town-and-the-immediate-outlying-district,' he said. 'And it's why we live in a palace like this.' He gestured to the gargantuan residence behind them. 'Because we are so brilliant, so instinctual. We are, in fact, a higher species ...'

At this, Nate looked around, beaming, and his chest puffed out until Artie thought it might pop the buttons on his shirt.

'*Ouch. Ouch. Ouch. Ouch.*'

Artie turned to see Funnel-web hobbling out to join them, being helped along by Mr Budgie. He was still covered head to foot in prickles the size of sewing needles.

'Gimme that!' he snarled, tearing Gareth from Artie's hands. 'Oh, so you like this little fella, do you? Well, let's see how you like him as a *frisbee*!' Artie stared in dismay as the hairy man began an awkward and painful little run-up in order to fling the unfortunate beast as far as he could.

'Ouch. Ouch. Ouch ouch ouch ouch.'

'Wait!' commanded the Mayor. 'We need this tortoise.'

Funnel-web halted, clearly disappointed.

'Since you fools have allowed the fat friend to escape, we are going to find a *substitute* for my feast.' The Mayor stared deep into Artie's eyes again. 'You are going to fetch us your little tortoise-loving girlfriend.'

Artie froze. He couldn't possibly let Gladys be dragged into this ordeal.

'I won't do it,' he said.

'Oh, yes you will,' the Mayor murmured. 'Or very much worse things will happen to you than merely being eaten by my family as a kebab.'

Artie briefly tried to imagine anything worse than being consumed by the Grime family, but came up with nothing.

'If you refuse to help us something dreadful might befall your *family*, and that would be a terrible outcome, wouldn't it?'

Artie gasped, and bit his lip to stop from crying, but had to bite it so hard that he felt he might actually chew it right off.

'Can I come please, Dad?' begged Nate. 'I can help! I'll show you where she lives!'

'Well, you'll have to ask your mother ...' said the Mayor. 'But she's working out at the moment, so I wouldn't want to bother her right now.'

Suddenly, above them, a window was flung open and a head appeared.

'What's all that booming and banging that's been going on?' screeched the face. It was a truly terrifying face. If Nate Grime would win a bronze medal in the Scary Olympics, and Mayor Grime silver, then Mrs Grime would win gold in a clean sweep across all categories.

Her dyed-black hair perched on her head like a stork's nest. She had a mouth like a cat-flap, and a gigantic jaw that appeared to be in need of a shave. She wore a sparkly lycra jumpsuit and her spray-tanned skin was the colour of an overripe tangerine.

'Sorry, Jaynee dear, nothing to worry about!' trilled Mr Grime with a tight little smile.

'I'm trying to lift weights here! And I've got a terrible migraine coming on. But does anybody care? Does anybody care?' she shrieked. She had a voice like a chainsaw.

'Yes, dear, I do, dear,' piped Mayor Grime meekly.

In that instant, Artie decided he had nothing to lose. He would appeal to Mrs Grime. Surely she would take pity on him!

'Please, Mrs Grime! Can you help me?' he called. 'I'm scared! I think Mr Grime is trying to … eat me!'

There was a silence, during which the huge face gazed blankly down at the small boy. Artie waited, his heart thumping. *She's going to save me*, he thought desperately … *She will save me!*

'Well, make sure you don't polish off the lot of him,' she bellowed. 'And I want the prime cuts, alright? No cheap cuts!'

'Of course, my nightingale!' cooed the Mayor. He pinched Artie hard on the arm for his insolence.

'Mummy?' called Nate.

'Yes, Natey-poo? My little poozy. My boozy-woozy. My boozy-woozy little woozy-poo ...' she crooned. Her neck bulged with muscles which rippled at every word, like death adders trying to escape from a rubber bag.

'Mummy, can I go with Dad and watch him at work today?'

'Well ... I suppose you can ... Anything that Natey wants Natey can have! But make sure you're not home too late so we can play some video games before bed. I've downloaded

SHOOT THEM, KILL THEM, STEAL THEIR CARS! 3·2,'

she squawked.

'Epic!' said Nate, punching the air.

The gruesome woman then turned to her husband. 'And make sure he eats something sensible before he goes out. There are a few leftover guinea-pig fillets from Sunday lunch and some cold poodle in a Tupperware in the fridge.'

'Yes, Jaynee dear, of course, dear.'

The horrifying face retreated and the window slammed shut.

'Right, *you!*' thundered the Mayor, giving Artie a shove. 'In the car! And bring that tortoise, boys!'

Chapter 24

Into the Unknown

'This is the place,' said Nate excitedly. 'This dump here. And that one next door is the slum where Farty Artie lives.'

Mary, who was driving (having bandaged his nose with a handkerchief held in place with an elastic band) brought the Rolls-Royce to a halt outside the Unpronounceable-enkos' house.

'Her parents are losers who talk funny,' Nate continued. 'And she's got a stupid name like Gladwrap or something ...'

'They're not losers!' protested Artie. He was sandwiched between Nate and Funnel-web in the back seat. 'They're really kind! And her name is Gladys, and it's a cool name!'

'Oooooooh!' cried Nate. 'Someone seems to be very touchy about his *girlfriend* ...'

'She's not my—' Artie stopped and stared at the floor. There was no point wasting his time bickering with Nate. He was beginning to feel that there was no point trying to fight *anything* anymore. He felt completely desolate. His only comfort was that if he did as he was told, the gang would leave his family alone, and that it seemed Bumshoe had escaped to safety with Aunty-boy.

Artie listened with tears in his eyes as Mayor Grime began to describe what Artie had to do. 'You will go to the front door and ask to see this Gladys and give her her tortoise. You will tell her that the wonderful Mayor Grime found him and returned him safely, and that she should come and thank me here at the car. When she does so, we shall be ready, shan't we, boys?'

'Oooh yeah!' 'Yes, Boss!' 'We'll be here!' agreed Nate, Mary and Funnel-web.

'And my banquet will once more be underway!' The Mayor's lips curled back. 'Of course, I needn't remind you what the penalty will be for any disobedience or tricks ...'

'No,' replied Artie in a tiny voice.

'That's right,' whispered the Mayor. 'We don't want to have to pay *your* house a visit as well ...'

Nate grinned. 'His mum's a loony who never gets out of her pyjamas and his sister always looks like she's about to smash something. Plus!' Nate began cackling. 'His dad was a circus clown! Probably died when some spinning plates landed on his head! Or maybe he fell off his unicycle!'

The gang exploded with laughter. Mayor Grime was doubled over, and looked as if he was about to choke. Long strands of oily hair uncoiled themselves from his bare scalp and flopped about.

'He wasn't a clown,' snapped Artie through his tears. 'He was a trapeze artist. And a tightrope walker. But he got sick. And he had more bravery in his little toe than you'll ever have.'

The Mayor stopped laughing. He patted his hairs back into place. Then he lunged towards Artie from the front seat, his face a pencil's width from the boy's. Artie blinked in terror.

'My son has more worth in *his* little toe than *you'll* ever have,' he seethed. 'Now I'm very hungry, so get out and get the girl, or the remnants of your family will be receiving a visit.'

Mortified at what he was about to do, but unable to see an escape from it, Artie slid out of the huge car, clutching the little tortoise. Mayor Grime stayed perched in the front passenger seat, but Mary, Funnel-web and Nate moved into the front garden, ready to pounce on Gladys when the time came.

Artie's mind felt as if it was moving at the speed of light. He trudged up the pathway towards the Unpronounceable-enkos' front door, shaking and sweating so much that Gareth almost slid out of his hands. He glanced back at the shapes of his tormentors as they ducked behind shrubs and trees in the garden.

For some reason, Artie was still thinking about his dad, and his saying that the best discoveries happen when you take a step into the unknown.

He arrived at Gladys's front door. Then he turned back to the street. He could see Mayor Grime in the car, furiously signalling at him to get a move on.

A step into the unknown, thought Artie. What did it mean?

He turned back to the door and lifted his hand to knock. *A step*, he thought. *Just a step.* Before he knew it, he was stepping swiftly across the verandah, away from the door. Then the steps spilt into a run!

He vaulted sideways over the railing, and took off down the side of the Unpronounceable-enkos' house. Finding his secret entrance through the tiny gap in the hedge with the broken fence palings, Artie was into his own backyard in seconds. He was faintly aware of Mary and Funnel-web bellowing and tearing up and down the Unpronounceable-enkos' driveway, trying to figure out where the skinny boy had got to. But

Artie was barrelling through the back door of his own house, slamming and locking it. Then he catapulted through to the front door, which he double-locked.

'What are you doing? And where have you been, you gherkin? You know you've had Mum worried sick, don't you?' It was Lola, screaming at him. Never had Artie been so overjoyed to see his furious sister.

'What makes you think you can stay away for as long as you like without letting Mum know? You're such a selfish ... You're a ...'

But the small boy had reached out to his sister and was holding her in a huge hug.

Artie's mum's bedroom door creaked open, and her sad, resigned face peered out.

'Oh, Artie, where have you been?' she sighed.

Artie could hear the voices of the gang calling to each other outside, still trying to hunt him down. He let go of Lola and took a deep breath. He was going to tell them the whole story.

'Mum, can you hear those voices?' He didn't wait for her answer. 'They're very bad men, who are in a gang … the gang I told you about with the Cave-of-Possibly-Stolen-Stuff that turned out to be Definitely-Stolen-Stuff and I know you didn't believe me about the cave but it's true and then Bumshoe and I tried to get proof but we lost Angus's camera and a man we call Mary on account of he's got Mary on his face stole it and he was going to the toilet but then he chased us with Funnel-web and then they caught Bumshoe in the washing machine and Nate's dad who's the mayor is in charge and they're robbing everybody and they stole Gareth the tortoise because the Mayor only eats pets because they're tender and then they caught me in the factory and took me up to Grime House where everything was made from gold and they were going to make skewers out of Bumshoe and me but then Aunty-boy snuck in with Macaroni dressed as statues and shot them with a Prickle-ator and the Fartex and we escaped but I wanted to save Gareth so I went back and a lizard ran over me and they caught me again and I thought Mrs Grime might help me but she's scarier than the lot of them and they tried to make me catch Gladys but I wouldn't do it and I know you'll never, never, ever believe me, but this time it's true and ...'

Here Artie paused. He realised what a complete mess he was making of his story. The more details he added, the more ridiculous it all seemed.

He sniffed, and tried to continue, but before he knew it his body was racked with sobs.

'And they're outside now and I have no idea what to do. And ... I want ... my mum. I want my mum.' Artie could speak no more. It was as if a dam wall was collapsing and flooding the room with tears.

Since the hugging incident, Lola had been silent, staring open-mouthed between Artie and her mum, Maggie, as if she was watching a really complicated game of tennis. She hadn't even looked at her phone once.

'As if!' she finally said. 'Mum, you don't believe him, do

you? You know what he's like …' But Lola didn't seem quite convinced by her own words.

Maggie Small knelt down in front of her son, staring at him.

'No. He's not – he's *not* lying,' she said quietly, and all at once she was reaching out for Artie and dragging him into her arms. She held him tightly and then, holding his face, she looked deeply into his eyes, blinking. It was as if she was coming out of a long, bad dream.

'Artie,' she whispered. 'Oh, my boy … My poor boy. How could I … What have I been doing? I'm so sorry.'

BOMPH BOMPH BOMPH BOMPH BOMPH

There was an almighty pounding on the front door, and the sound of a window smashing. Lola screamed.

Maggie was across the room like a flash.

From her bedroom came the sound of cupboard doors being flung open. In seconds she emerged. Artie and Lola were amazed – for years they had only ever seen her shuffling about in her dressing-gown and slippers.

But here she was, wearing jeans and a T-shirt, and with a look of barely contained rage in her eyes.

The pounding became even more insistent, as if the front door was about to be pummelled off its hinges.

'RIGHT!' Maggie bellowed.

'THAT'S IT!'

Chapter 25

Golf

Maggie Small tore open the skinny cupboard beside the front door and came out wielding one of her old golf clubs, which had not seen the light of day since Artie's dad died.

Without pausing, she threw open the front door and walked straight into Mary, Funnel-web and Nate, who were at that moment attempting to kick the door in, and caught them completely off-guard.

Her voice was guttural and low, like some kind of African animal's. *'You dare! You dare to lay a finger on ... MY BOY?'* Maggie growled. **'Well???'**

There was a slack-jawed silence from the gang members.

THWACK!!!

Maggie brought
the golf club
crashing down
onto Mary's toes.

'WHAAAAAAAAAAAA-AAAAAAAAAAAAAAAA-AAAAAAAAAAAH ...'

he bleated, and began leaping about on one leg. Clutching his nose (which was still bandaged from Macaroni's assault) with one hand, and his squashed foot with the other, the enormous man took off, hopping away out of the yard.

'I said, do you *dare* to lay ... a *finger* ... on *my boy*?' Maggie seethed, staring wild-eyed at the two remaining at the door.

Funnel-web shuffled his feet and looked about, plucking at a couple of prickles on his cheek, and then he and Nate turned as one and bolted as fast as they could for the front gate.

But Maggie Small was not finished. Not by a long way. She flew after them, swinging her golf club at their rear ends.

Artie, with Lola behind him, followed his mum out onto the street and watched in growing delight as Funnel-web and Nate piled into the back seat of the Rolls-Royce, locking the doors. Mayor Grime began berating them from the front.

'I give you *one simple task!*' he blustered. 'And what do you do? You cretins! You complete *cretins.*' He turned to Nate. 'And you!' he lamented. 'My own flesh and blood …'

BOPH!!!

Maggie bashed the golf club hard down over the roof, just above Mayor Grime's head. His tiny eyes nearly popped out of his face.

'Are you mad?' he roared from behind the glass. 'Don't you know who I am?'

'Yes,' said Maggie in an eerie, even tone. 'I believe you are the Mayor. It's lovely to meet you.'

With that Maggie smashed Mayor Grime's windscreen to

smithereens, and calmly strolled around the shiny vehicle, smashing every window that remained. Then, standing at the front of the car as if lining up for a golf stroke, she demolished first one headlight, then the other.

'You dare ... lay a finger ... on my boy?' she repeated as she walked around to the back, warming to her task.

Artie could hear the Mayor, who by this time was cowering on the floor, bellowing for someone to start the car and get them out of there. Unfortunately for him, it was Mary who had the car keys, and Mary was at that moment still nursing his toes and nose, peeking out from behind a nearby shrub.

Artie and Lola stood watching in jubilation as Maggie Small totally destroyed a spanking-new Rolls-Royce with a nine iron.

'Cool!' whispered Lola, who now had her trusty phone out and was filming the entire episode.

'Epic!' said Artie. He wished that Bumshoe was with him to witness the sheer fabulousness of this moment.

'Whew!!' exclaimed Maggie, pausing for a moment to wipe a strand of hair from her eyes and admire her handiwork. 'Not used to all this exercise!'

She turned and beamed at her children.

Artie felt tears rushing to his eyes. He hadn't seen his mum smile for years.

'ARGH. ARGH. ARGH.'

During the brief cessation of the assault, Mary had taken the opportunity to sprint to the car (as best he could on his damaged foot), and was prising the driver's door open.

He leapt in, stuck his head out of where the windscreen used to be, gunned the engine and tried to take off. A meteor shower of broken glass flew up in the wrecked car's wake and the tailpipe dragged along the road behind it, sending up a barrage of sparks.

Maggie trotted behind the car for a little, smashing its rear end every now and then as it tried to escape, till finally, spluttering and growling, the broken Rolls-Royce picked up enough speed to roar off down the road.

'Well!' she said, returning to her children. 'It's nice to play a little golf again ...'

Chapter 26

A Bit of a Mission

'C'mon!' urged Maggie over her shoulder. Artie and Lola followed sheepishly behind her as she tore up the front stairs of Gladys's house, still wielding her golf club.

'What are you doing, Mum?' called Artie.

Although both Artie and Lola were over the moon that their mother appeared to have come back to life, they were also a little worried about where all this might be leading.

'We haven't even started yet!' Maggie pronounced, knocking firmly on the Unpronounceable-enkos' front door.

The door was shortly opened by Gladys. She took in the bizarre vision of Maggie Small, dressed in day clothes and holding a golf club, and then turned to Artie.

Before he knew it, Gladys was leaping towards him, squealing in delight. Artie had forgotten he'd been clutching Gareth under his arm the whole time!

'Gareth! Where did you find him?' cried the delighted girl, dancing around with her little tortoise.

'Well, um, you see ...' began Artie, but he was cut off mid-sentence as Gladys began kissing him all over his face.

'Thank you, Artie! Thank you! Thank you!'

Artie's eyes nearly fell on the floor. Being kissed by Gladys was freaky, and also a bit nice, but it did make his face once again turn the colour of Zoran's beetroot soup.

Oksana, Zoran and the twins arrived at the door. The parents stared open-mouthed at Maggie, as if seeing a phantom.

'Erm … Mrs Small! How lovely to …' Oksana finally said. 'Erm … Would you like to come in?'

'I know you probably hardly remember me, but please, call me Maggie. Oksana, I have a strange request: would you mind very much if I borrowed your car? Just for a little bit?'

Oksana and Zoran glanced at one another and then exchanged a few words in Ukrainian.

'Of course … Maggie,' said Oksana. 'Is there anything wrong?'

'Is there something I can help with?' enquired Zoran at the same time.

'No. You're very kind, but I'm on a bit of a mission, you see? This is something *I* need to do,' Maggie replied.

'Mum,' Artie interjected. 'It might be a good idea if Zoran comes along. He's very … *useful*.'

'Oh, yes!' exclaimed Zoran with a huge grin. 'I'm very useful!'

'Can I come too?' said Gladys.

And before Oksana could say no, they were all leaping into Zoran's old car.

Maggie paused for a moment.

'Zoran,' she said. 'If you don't mind, I'd really love to *drive*!'

Chapter 27

The Leaning Tower of Bumshoes

Maggie hurtled through the streets of town, squealing around corners, tooting the horn and roaring past cars. Artie sat beside her, shouting out directions to Grime House. He turned to glance at the passengers in the back. Lola and Gladys looked a little queasy, but Zoran seemed remarkably relaxed.

'This is how everyone drive in Ukraine!' he yelled. 'It's like I'm *home* again!'

As they drove, Artie filled Zoran and Gladys in on what had befallen him and Bumshoe at the hands of the Grime gang.

Zoran shook his big head in astonishment.

'I'm very sorry we didn't believe that story when you tell us at first, Artie! It just seem … like maybe you making up some little porky pies!'

'That's okay,' said Artie. 'I have been known to cry wolf sometimes … Mum! Sharp right at the next corner!'

Artie grinned. He felt like a navigator in a rally-car championship. He realised he was having *fun* ... Proper, world championship, completely illegal *fun*!

He turned around to look at Lola, who, although terrified at their mum's driving, had an excited smile on her face. She had her phone out the window and was filming everything. She met Artie's eyes, and they began to giggle. Lola looked like a completely different person.

The car began to climb the steep hill into the posh part of town. Maggie was sitting forward, her hands clenched on the wheel, her foot to the floor, willing the Unpronounceable-enkos' old car to get up the hill faster.

At last they skidded to a stop outside Grime House in a great plume of dust, and leapt out of the car. The electric gates, which looked as high as a circus tent, were shut tight, and there was no sign of life. Artie peered through the bars. A little distance away on a grassy mound perched the two guards who were supposed to be manning the entrance. They were covered head to foot in prickles, and were delicately picking them off each other. They looked like a pair of chimps at the zoo. Artie smiled. There was no doubt how Aunty-boy and Bumshoe had made their escape!

Just then there was a loud groaning engine noise coming up the road, and roaring to a halt right beside them was the Bumshoe family in their big old converted school bus. Bumshoe was the first of millions to leap out.

'Artie!' he called, running to his friend. 'I've been worried sick about you! I'm glad you're not a kebab!'

Artie was about to enquire about Aunty-boy when Angus, Bumshoe's big brother, clambered down from the driver's seat. He looked very worried.

'Ah! Mrs Small … Have you heard about everything that's happened?' he asked. 'Apparently it all started when the boys nicked my camera—'

'Well, *technically* we borrowed it…' corrected Bumshoe.

'*No, technically* you nicked it. And *technically* I'd like to get it back!' replied Angus.

Before the argument between the two brothers could go any further, Maggie was moving over to the intercom system at the gate. 'Oh, yes, I've heard all about it,' she said, pressing the buzzer.

After a moment a sound crackled over the speaker. 'The Grime residence. Ow. How may I be of assistance? Ow …' came the voice that Artie at once recognised as Funnel-web, (and obviously still suffering the after-effects of the Prickle-ator).

'It's Artie Small's mother here! I'd like to come up and talk to the Mayor!' said Maggie tersely at the intercom.

'I'm terribly sorry but the Grime family – ow – is currently on vacation in St Tropez. Ow … May I take a message?'

'No, you may not,' said Maggie. 'I'm going to deliver *my* message in person.'

'I'm afraid that won't be possible, you see—'

But Maggie had already given up on the intercom and was tugging at the bars on the humungous gate. These were made of thick steel, and even with her apparent new super-powers, the gate wouldn't budge.

Bumshoe poked his friend in the ribs and shook a packet of Chococaramel-Cococreambombs at him. 'Oi! What's with yer mum? When'd she get out of bed?'

'Incredible, right?' grinned Artie, with a shrug.

'Alright!' shouted Maggie to the assembled crowd. 'Who's got some *rope*?'

Everyone looked about, shaking their heads.

'Okay, here's what's going to happen! You're all going to take off your jumpers and tie them sleeve to sleeve! And *tight knots*, please!' she yelled.

Within seconds the assembled crew had tied all their jumpers together in one long jumper-rope, and everyone was wondering what was going to happen next.

'Now! Who knows what a human pyramid is?' called Maggie.

'Oh, yeah, we know that, Mrs S!' cried Bumshoe excitedly. 'We do them all the time at home, when we have to clean the gutters on the roof and stuff, 'cause we can never find the ladder!'

'It's true!' announced Angus. 'We're actually pretty good at these things—'

'This is how we do it, Mrs S,' explained Bumshoe, strolling over to her. 'My big brothers Angus, Travis, Nicky, Tom, Jarrod, Willy and Sam make a circle like this, with arms around each other's shoulders. And then Ava, Chloe, Kieren, Rufus and myself climb up to form the next layer, and following—'

'I'm really sorry, dear,' said Maggie. 'But I'm in a bit of a *rush* … Would you mind just *showing* me?'

'Oh, yeah, of course, Mrs S!' smiled Bumshoe. 'Come on, gang!' he bellowed.

In a gale of excited chatter, the vast squad of Bumshoe siblings, most of whom were of very ample proportions, belted over to the gate, and in double-quick time were constructing a great tower of Bumshoes.

'So … erm … what's next, Mrs S?' came the muffled voice of Artie's friend from inside the pyramid.

'Brace yourselves, kids!' yelled Maggie. Taking a few steps backwards, and clutching the rope of jumpers, she sprinted full-tilt towards the group, leapt onto the pyramid and scuttled all the way to the top. Luckily for the Bumshoes, she was as light as a feather from having hardly eaten for so many years. When she was balanced at the apex, she reached over and lifted herself onto the top of the gate, where she perched precariously.

'Be careful, Maggie, for goodness-gracious sake!' yelled Zoran.

'Yeah, Mum, be careful, please!' implored Artie.

Hauling up the heavy rope of jumpers, she tied one end to the top of the gate, and flung the rest of it over the other side to the ground.

'Alright!' she cried. 'Thanks, team! You can *de-pyramid* now!'

'WAIT! MUM!!!' yelled Artie.

In a flash, he too was scrabbling up over the now-leaning-tower-of-Bumshoes. He dragged himself up to sit beside his mother.

'Alright,' Artie called. '*Now* you can de-pyramid!'

Instantly, the tower of brothers and sisters began to collapse, giggling and yelping. Artie stared straight ahead to avoid the sick feeling at being suspended so far up in the air.

He allowed himself a glance at the two guards but they were still so busy picking needles off each other that they had barely noticed the commotion unfolding at the gate.

Maggie reached over and wrapped her arm around Artie's shoulders, squeezing him.

'Are you alright?' she whispered.

Artie nodded.

'Do you know who you reminded me of just now?'

Artie, staring at the horizon, shook his head.

'Your dad,' she said.

'Really?' exclaimed Artie, turning to her, a grin spreading over his face.

'*So much!*' smiled his mum.

Despite being so far off the ground, Artie realised that he was beginning to feel quite relaxed. Way down below, the crowd looked on in worried silence.

'Shall we?' said Maggie.

'Yes,' said Artie.

Then, grasping the rope of jumpers tightly, Maggie gently dropped from the top, and lowered herself to the ground.

At the bottom, she looked up at her son and nodded. Artie took a deep breath. He held the jumper-rope with all his strength, wriggled carefully around and tried to lower himself. He dropped. The makeshift rope took the strain, and he swung wildly for a moment like a pendulum, his heart in his mouth. Then, his muscles straining, he began climbing down.

As he landed safely beside his mum there was a spontaneous clap and whoop of relief from the little crowd outside the gate.

'Well done, Artie!' cried Bumshoe.

'Good work! Good work!' called Zoran.

Maggie Small held Artie's face in her hands, beaming.

'Brave boy,' she said. 'Now. Let's go!'

Chapter 28

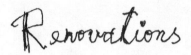

Renovations

Lola, Angus, Zoran, Gladys and the rest of the Bumshoes were excitedly chattering outside the gate, when over the hubbub came the sound of an engine screaming at full throttle.

'LOOK OUT, KIDS!' yelled Angus.

Careering backwards down the driveway and coming directly towards them was Mayor Grime's battered Rolls-Royce. It was travelling at an insane speed, with blue smoke billowing out of the engine. Rather than slowing down as it approached the gates, the car accelerated even more. The crowd leapt for their lives in all directions.

WHOOOOOOOOOOOMP!!!

It crashed right through, destroying the entire structure and leaving broken bits and twisted metal everywhere. The unfortunate vehicle stopped in the street.

There at the wheel was Maggie Small, with Artie goggle-eyed beside her.

'Lucky someone left the keys in the ignition!' said Maggie, with a little smile. 'Hope I didn't scare anyone!'

She revved the engine and roared back through the smashed gate. Angus, dusting himself off, turned to the rest of the group. 'Well … Now that we've been … erm … granted admission … all aboard, I guess.'

Everyone clambered into the Bumshoe family bus, which lumbered through the huge gap where the gates had stood and up the hill towards Grime House.

Meanwhile, what remained of Mayor Grime's Rolls-Royce was speeding ahead up the driveway.

'What exactly are we going to do, Mum?' cried Artie. 'These are really, really scary people ...'

Maggie looked at him for a brief moment, and then stomped on the brakes. The car slid sideways to a halt.

'Artie,' she said. 'I'm so *angry!*'

'Yeah, um, I did notice that, Mum ...'

'I'm really, *really* angry! I think, maybe, when your dad died, I needed to get angry back then, but I just got ... shocked instead, and I kind of ... stayed shocked, and maybe all the anger got stuck inside me and could never come out and—'

'Mum,' said Artie.

'Yes, Artie?'

'It's really great having you back.'

Maggie gave a little smile.

'Seatbelt!' she said, briskly. 'We've got some more renovations to do for the Grime family ...'

Artie gulped and clipped on his belt, as Maggie thundered off. The imposing shape of Grime House loomed on the horizon.

Rather than slowing down, however, Maggie Small, for the

second time that day, seemed intent on driving into something. She began accelerating towards the house.

As they neared the monstrous structure, Artie noticed that Mary and Funnel-web had strolled out onto the front steps to see what all the hullabaloo was about. Maggie was hurtling straight at them.

'Mum,' said Artie. 'Mum ... Mum ... MUM ... MUM!!!'

Artie could see the terror in the robbers' eyes as they parted and dived out of the way.

Mounting the great marble steps that led up to the house, the car became airborne …

KER-BAAAAAAAAAASH!!

They ploughed right through the front doors and into the grand foyer, in a storm of splinters and bricks.

There was silence all around. A puff of plasterwork slowly drifted down onto their heads as Artie and Maggie climbed out of the tangled mess that used to be the Grime family car.

'Well,' Maggie exclaimed. 'It's wonderful that the Mayor makes himself so available to the public. This really is democracy at work!'

'Grab them! Get them! I want both of them in cages!!!'

Artie gasped. It was the Mayor himself, who at that moment was materialising from a hallway with Mr Budgie.

'YOU!' thundered Maggie, staring him into immediate silence. 'My son has told me all about *you* …' she continued very quietly, slowly advancing on him.

The Mayor, petrified, began to retreat.

'Well, do something, you ridiculous birdcage person!' he screeched at Mr Budgie.

'Alright … I will,' said the little man, and with that he tore the cage clean off his head and flung it away. He shrugged at Artie.

'That's better. Never liked this gang anyway,' he said. 'I'm going back to science teaching.' As Mr Budgie wandered off, Mary and Funnel-web entered, limping and shaking dust off themselves.

Maggie, still staring at the Mayor, grabbed the first useful object she could see, which happened to be a pot plant. Armed with this, she sprang at him and began whacking him over and over again.

THWACK. 'AAARGH!' *THWACK.* 'AAARGH!' *THWACK.* 'AAARGH!'

The Mayor shrieked and tried to dart out of her way. But Maggie was not about to stop. As he scuttled over the debris and through the remains of the door, she was right behind him, beating his bottom mercilessly with the potted palm. They disappeared into the garden.

Just then, Artie felt a claw-like hand clutch him at the back of the neck.

'Oh. You'll pay for this ...' whispered a voice he knew to be Funnel-web's.

Chapter 29

UKRAINIAN OLYMPIC DISCUS CHAMPION, 1996

Artie cowered, paralysed with fear. Then, ahead of him, Mary's enraged face loomed out of the plaster-dust.

'Let's get him in one of those cages, Funnel-web,' he breathed.

But then the icy talon gripping Artie's neck was suddenly torn away. The boy turned to find Zoran, who had plucked Funnel-web up by his shirt and pants and was casually holding him sideways off the ground.

Then, using the spidery man's head as a battering-ram, Zoran charged full-tilt towards Mary, clomping him right in his enormous belly.

'OOOOOOOOOPH,' came a strange noise from the tattooed man, like a tractor tyre exploding, as he sailed backwards into a wall.

Zoran, who still held on to Funnel-web, turned to Artie.

'Now I show you how Zoran became Ukrainian Olympic Discus Champion, 1996!'

With that, he began to spin the hairy man around and around.

'No. Stop it ... Pleeeeeease. I get dreadful motion- sickness ... Pleeeeeease,' Funnel-web pleaded, to no avail.

Spiralling at an extraordinary Ukrainian-Olympic-record-breaking speed, Zoran let go at last, and watched with Artie as Funnel-web soared through the air, and smashed right through a plate-glass window.

'Aaaaaaaaaaaaaaaaaaaargh!'

There was a little thud in the distance, followed by a tiny, 'Ow.'

Artie, elated, had no doubt how Zoran had won all his medals. The huge man turned to him, beaming.

'I still got it, huh? Once a Ukrainian Olympic Discus Champion, 1996, *always* a Ukrainian Olympic Discus Champion, 1996!'

Zoran paused and plucked at one of his palms.

'Ouch! He got prickles, that one!'

Then the discus champion grinned and added, 'Now I better go and rescue the Mayor from your mama!'

He rushed out into the garden. During all of this, the entrance foyer of Grime House had been overrun by Bumshoes, who had gleefully disembarked from the bus as if they were on a school excursion. Mary gingerly picked himself up off the ground and tried to sneak out into the garden, but quickly found himself surrounded by clusters of the siblings. Every time he turned to flee, a Bumshoe would park himself on all fours behind him, and he'd trip head-first into the dust. This went on at length until finally the villain, exhausted and forlorn, decided to stay flat on the floor for safety.

'AAAAARROOOOOOO!'

A bloodcurdling howl silenced the room. Artie spun around to see the two men in sunglasses emerging from the hallway. In front of them, straining at a thick chain, was Tinkerbell.

The fearsome animal looked even bigger than Artie recalled. He snapped and lunged towards the crowd, who recoiled in horror.

Trails of slobber leaked from his jaws, which stretched back to reveal gigantic yellow fangs.

'Ooh, look!' cried Mary, who, with renewed confidence, was once again standing. 'Look at Artie's face! Someone doesn't seem to like Tinkerbell, does he?'

'Don't hurt him!' commanded a voice. Artie swung around to see Gladys, stepping forward. 'You'll only end up going to jail for longer!' she exclaimed. 'Don't you see? We're all witnesses!'

'Yes, we're all witnesses!' It was Lola, who also stepped forward, holding her phone aloft. 'And I'm getting all of this on film. So you better back away from my brother!'

'You're only witnesses until the moment you're all torn to pieces by a wild dog,' said Mary with a dry laugh.

The two henchmen stared through their sunglasses like gargantuan insects.

'AAAAAARROOOOOOOOOOO!'

The dog was pulling ever closer to Artie.

'Easy, boy … Easy …' whispered his handler, as he leaned down. Then, aiming his expressionless face at Artie, he unclipped the hound's chain.

'Now get them all,' he growled. The hulking animal, his massive mouth wide open, lurched forward directly at Artie's neck!

BLAAAAAAT-BLAT-BLAT-PLAAARP!!!

The hound suddenly skittered sideways. He tried to stay upright but kept slipping about in custardy goop, as a torrent of thick yellow slime was blown about the room.

Artie, still in shock at having nearly become Tinkerbell's chew-toy, turned in bewilderment.

There, in the wreckage of the doorway, was Aunty-boy with her Super-Snotter!

Chapter 30

Flu-Snot

The old lady was wearing the canister of the machine strapped to her back, and was hopping around, thrusting her dentures out, and waggling the nozzle of the Super-Snotter as if she was putting out a house fire.

'Oooh, yes, I'm very happy with that!' she warbled. 'Yes, that's working much better than the early trials.'

To cries of delight from the Bumshoe family, she focused the stream onto Mary and the men in sunglasses as they tried to run away. They splashed, slipped and crawled about in the snotty mire.

Artie observed that on contact with air, the disgusting substance quickly thickened up, becoming more like really nasty flu-snot than watery hayfever-snot. He and Gladys noticed a pool of it slowly oozing towards their feet, and climbed the stairs to escape it.

'Artie!' bellowed Bumshoe. 'We've gotta get a couple of these things!'

Catching eyes with his friend, Artie burst out laughing and for the first time since stumbling onto the cave of stolen stuff, he began to believe that things might actually, incredibly, turn out alright.

The room was a scene of mayhem, as the Bumshoes urged Aunty-boy on and yelled when Mary, Tinkerbell, or the men in sunglasses were struggling free, at which point Aunty-boy would take aim and give them a fresh squirt of the mucus-y gunk.

Gradually, the entire gang became completely stuck, wriggling in the viscous ooze until they were utterly immobilised. Macaroni, who had been waiting at his mistress's feet, began scampering around the edges of the giant snot puddle, nipping at any stray limb that made the mistake of popping out. Artie and Gladys climbed higher up the stairs to get a perfect view of the crazy scene below.

At that moment Maggie and Zoran arrived back at the entrance. Maggie was breathless from her work spanking Mayor Grime around the garden.

'Wow!' cried Zoran. 'I don't know how sorry Mr Mayor is for

being bad. But I think Mr Mayor's bottom is very, very sorry!'

'Pheeeew!' panted Maggie, and grabbing hold of Lola, squeezed her daughter tight. 'I'm loving all this exercise! Have I missed anything?'

'Um … well …' said Lola. 'I'm not sure where to begin. I can show you a video if you like!'

At this moment, Artie thought he felt something grasp his ankle, but ignored it, distracted by the hilarious spectacle of the snot-covered criminals. Then, suddenly, his world was turned upside-down.

'OIII!!!' came a voice like a jackhammer.

The entire room looked up to see Mrs Grime standing on a landing at the top of the staircase, looming above the entrance foyer. Beside her stood Nate, who surveyed the scene below with undisguised contempt.

'NOW, THAT GOT YER ATTENTION!' smiled the musclebound ogress.

With superhuman strength, she was holding Artie and Gladys by the ankles, dangling them upside down over the edge of the balcony.

Chapter 31

The Flying Trapeze

'Honestly!' whined Mrs Grime. 'I'm sick to death of this! If I want any job done properly around this place it's always down to *me*!'

Maggie stood staring, holding her breath. Zoran, who was usually so courageous, was as white as paper. Nobody moved in case the terrible woman suddenly let go and sent Artie and Gladys plummeting to their deaths.

Artie, upside down and face-to-face with Gladys, tried to console the stricken girl. 'Gladys! It's going to be okay!' he whispered, although in truth he had no idea of how it would be okay.

In an instant, Aunty-boy swung the nozzle of the Super-Snotter straight up at Mrs Grime, and was reaching for the trigger.

'Don't even think about it, crazy lady!'

206

the woman roared at Aunty-boy. 'Take that machine off and chuck it away, or these kids find out all about gravity … the hard way!'

Nate, beside her, burst into wild laughter. 'Natey-poo, go down and get that thing off her, will you, darling?' The boy, still cackling, scampered all the way down the stairs, through the silent crowd, and wrenched the Super-Snotter out of Aunty-boy's hands, giving the old lady a nasty shove for good measure. Aunty-boy toppled backwards, barely managing to stay upright. Macaroni bared his teeth and leapt at the boy. 'Statue!' ordered Aunty-boy, and the dog immediately lay down, glowering at Nate, who strapped the canister of the Super-Snotter onto his back.

'Now! All of yez! Get out of my house! Go on! Get! Or these kids' heads are going to look like pancakes!!!'

'Please … Please don't hurt them!' said Maggie.

'Don't drop them!! Please, lady! Don't hurt them!!' implored Zoran.

'Please-don't-drop-them! Nya-nya-nya-nya!' mimicked Mrs Grime. 'Go on, I told yez! Get out!' she continued. 'WHOOOOOOOOA!!!' For a moment she pretended to let Artie slip. 'Almost dropped him! Hahaha! Should have seen your faces!!!' She roared with laughter, joined by Nate, who was now parading through the crowd below threatening everybody with the Super-Snotter. Suddenly Mrs Grime became deadly serious.

'That's yer last warning. I'm gonna count to three. ONE! TWO!—'

'What can we do?' whispered Gladys frantically.

'We can step into the unknown,' Artie replied.

'I don't know what you mean!'

'Nor do I. Yet,' said Artie.

Way below them, Maggie Small was desperate.

'What kind of mother are you?' she implored.

'Me?' squawked Mrs Grime. 'What kind of mother are *you*? Oh, yes, Natey's told me all about you ... Locked away for years, lying around in yer jim-jams doing nothin'!'

'Yeah!' snarled Nate. 'You just lie around all day! And that's why you live in such a dump!' he added, his microscopic eyes glinting with pleasure as he waggled the nozzle of the Super-Snotter in Maggie's face.

'Yes! It's true!' said Maggie Small, pushing the nozzle away. 'It's true! I've been a *terrible* mother, and I'll never forgive myself ...'

'No you haven't, Mum,' called Artie, as he dangled above. 'You're a great mum!'

'I'm not! I haven't been!' said Maggie, her eyes brimming with tears. 'I got lost somewhere ... But I'll make it up to you, Artie. Promise!'

'Nothing to make up, Mum!' replied Artie. 'All good, really!'

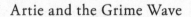

'WELL! I'm sorry to butt in on your little fairytale ending, guys, but my arms are getting a bit TIRED!!!' screeched the bulging harpy. Artie's mind was racing. Surely he hadn't survived all these crazy adventures only to be dropped on his head by a psycho muscle-lady! But he could see no solution. He could see nothing … nothing, except … his dad's pendant, which at that moment dangled down, right in front of his nose. Trapeze artists, one swinging from the other's arms …*Step into the unknown!* he thought. In one movement, he slipped the necklace over his head, and with an almighty jerk, he flicked himself up.

'RABBITS!!!' he bawled, and at

the same time he spun the necklace around Jaynee Grime's huge hand, lassoing it to his own ankle.

'What the—' The musclebound woman was momentarily befuddled.

Artie swung straight back down.

'Take my wrists!' he cried to Gladys.

The petrified girl grabbed at Artie.

'Right, I've had enough!!!' snarled the monstrous lady. And with a flourish, she released her grip and let the two children plummet to their deaths.

The end

Not really, dear reader...

The moment that
Jaynee Grime tried to
let go, she realised her
wrist was shackled tight
to Artie's ankle. She
couldn't let go of him!
Meanwhile, Gladys
tumbled, screaming, but
Artie grasped hold of her
wrists. For a brief time, the
two of them precisely resembled the
tiny figurines of Artie's dad's pendant.

Mrs Grime was now doubled over
the edge of the railing, the combined
weight of the children dragging her
down. The chain binding her to
Artie's ankle tore at her hand.
'AAAARGH. AAAARGH.
SOMEBODY HELP ME.
GET THEM OFF ME.
I'M STUCK ... HEEEEEEELP!!!'

In seconds, Maggie and Zoran arrived at the top of the stairs. Yanking hard on Mrs Grime, they forced her backwards until Artie slid up over the railing, bringing Gladys with him.

All of them collapsed in a huge heap on top of the herculean woman.

'GET ORF ME! ALL OF YEZ!!!'

yowled Mrs Grime.

But Maggie was sprawled out and holding on to Artie as though she would never let him go again.

'Mum … Mum! That's actually hurting … quite a lot,' he finally protested.

Zoran, meanwhile, seemed to be sobbing and laughing at the same time, and gripping Gladys in a huge bear hug, completely oblivious to the fact that he was squatting with his immense bottom perched on Mrs Grime's cheek.

'GET ORF ME!!!' came a muffled croak.

At that moment, way below them, Nate Grime decided to take matters into his own hands. He lifted the nozzle of the Super-Snotter, aimed it directly at Aunty-boy and Macaroni, and pulled the trigger.

BLAAT-BLAT-BLAT-PLAARP!!!

The machine blew a fat torrent of snot straight back into his own face. Artie looked on from the balcony as Nate, yelping and spluttering, seemed unable to switch the Super-Snotter off. It continued to spray him as he ducked and jigged all around the room, until it eventually appeared to run dry, by which time Nate Grime, curled in a corner and coated head to foot in congealing yellow slime, resembled a humungous booger.

Artie turned to Aunty-boy in amazement.

'How did you *do* that?' he asked.

'Well, one never invents a weapon without an emergency reverse-switch, does one, cherry puffs!' called the old lady. And with that, she clacked out her dentures and waddled out of the building, her faithful canine trotting along behind her.

In the distance came the sound of police sirens. Up on the balcony, and still crouching on Mrs Grime's head, Zoran let go of Gladys long enough to say, 'Has someone called the polices?'

At that moment, Lola arrived at the top of the stairs. She held her phone up.

'Oh, everything's already online. I've uploaded videos of the whole shebang to all the emergency services. They'll be here in…' she glanced at her phone, 'about two minutes,' she said brightly.

Maggie beamed as Lola came over to hug her, flopping down with the others on top of Mrs Grime.

'Get off me. I told yez...' came the feeble voice beneath them.

Gladys turned and gazed deeply into Artie's eyes.

'Thank you,' she said, simply.

Artie Small felt as if his heart might burst.

Chapter 32

And Then What Happened?

Well, I imagine, dear reader, that you're thinking this is the part where we talk about how perfect everything was for Artie Small from that moment on. The truth is, very much like life itself, there were pros and cons to Artie's new world...

Mayor Grime, Mrs Grime, and *the Grime Gang* went to prison for a very, very long time.

Nate Grime was sent to live with an aunt who was, by all accounts, very dull and very strict.

Maggie Small, who had hardly spoken a word for so many years, now would not stop talking! Having not spoken at all about Artie's dad since he died, Maggie was now forever telling stories about him. It was as if a fire hydrant of words had burst and was spraying the world in general, and Artie and Lola in particular, with endless thoughts and comments. This was wonderful, but sometimes the brother and sister really had to take a stroll outside for a bit of peace and quiet.

Since Artie's dad died, the very mention of him had been all but forbidden in the Small house. But now, the Small family lounge room was decorated with dozens of framed photos of him performing his feats of daring in the circus.

The Unpronounceable-enkos, who the whole town now knew as the Zatserklyannaya-Tsekmistrenkos, would visit Artie and his family for dinner every Sunday night, along with Aunty-boy, Macaroni and Bumshoe, with his brother Angus. Once, Maggie made the mistake of inviting the entire Bumshoe clan to one of these nights. It was as if the house had been overrun by a particularly cheerful invading army. Everything in the house that could be eaten was eaten, and even some things that should not, as Maggie noted with alarm when she saw that every bar of soap had disappeared, the pencils looked shorter, and the flower arrangement seemed to have been trimmed.

Maggie tended to oversee these dinners because she claimed Artie still had quite a lot to learn about flavour combinations. Macaroni would sit under the table and Artie would feed the dog little tidbits.

The best thing about these nights was that Artie could sit next to Gladys. Sometimes she would take his hand under the table, which was a bit *freaky*. In a nice sort of way.

Lola stopped yelling and stomping around the place, and began making documentaries with Angus Bumshoe. One of these, entitled *Artie and the Grime Wave*, told the entire story of Artie's adventures at the hands of the Grime family, and won numerous awards. After that, rather than putting up with Lola's anger anymore, Artie now just had to put up with her swanning about thinking that she was *the best thing ever*. But Artie did put up with it. Because Lola was happy. And secretly, that made Artie happy too.

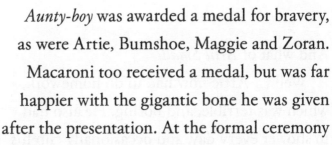

Aunty-boy was awarded a medal for bravery, as were Artie, Bumshoe, Maggie and Zoran. Macaroni too received a medal, but was far happier with the gigantic bone he was given after the presentation. At the formal ceremony at Government House, Aunty-boy clacked her false teeth out at the governor.

'Would you care to see my Fartex?' she enquired, and offered him a powder lolly. The worried governor was quickly ushered away by his security detail.

Bumshoe hand-delivered his Christmas present to Artie that year. Unwrapping it, Artie at first had no idea about the two weird objects sitting in the cardboard box in front of him. But then a huge smile spread over his face, and soon he was falling about with laughter.

'What on *earth* are they?' enquired Maggie, peering over their shoulders, bewildered.

'Paperbark shoes,' said the boys together, and they burst out laughing once again.

'It's a long story ...' Artie explained.

And what of *Artie Small*?

Well ... Artie now had to do homework, which was terrible, and boring. He also had to shower every day, and occasionally clip his toenails rather than letting them die of old age, as he was accustomed to. But complain as he might, there was no escaping any of it... his mum seemed to be very particular about these things. Maggie also insisted on taking him shopping for clothes, and he would pretend to be bored to death (he was twelve years old, after all!). But in fact, he was so relieved and happy to have his mum back that he really didn't mind. He didn't mind at all.

The end
(Really, this time)

Acknowledgements

I'd like to thank Louise Schwartzkopf and Monique Farmer at *Spectrum* magazine in the *Sydney Morning Herald,* who for reasons best known to themselves gave me an opportunity to write publicly for the first time.

Thank you to my literary agent, Grace Heifetz at Curtis Brown, for the many funny phone calls, and her unstinting good advice, and good taste.

Thanks to all the good people at Allen and Unwin, and special thanks to my editor, Anna McFarlane, for challenging me, making *Artie* better, and for helping me understand that there may feasibly be a limit to the number of gratuitous fart jokes a novel can withstand. Who knew?

Liz Seymour, the designer, who was somehow able to work with both my innumeracy and illegible scrawls, and fashion such beautiful pages.

Thank you to Kate Whitfield, my copy editor, who managed to hack her way through my jungle of dangling modifiers, and always come up with a better, clearer, simpler, less chaotic, more organised, less repetitive idea with fewer repetitions or commas, or repetitions, or indeed other punctuation points, than, for instance, I might have used otherwise.

Thanks to Mona Vale Library, where the bulk of *Artie* was dreamed of and written. What a joyous, bustling hub. What a testament to our civilisation!

There are not many places on earth that afford the opportunity to be stared at by water-dragons while working. Mona Vale Library is one of them. When I am the President of Australia my first act will be to ensure that every town and village has such a delightful community resource.

Thank you to Raphael and Miro Roxburgh. For blessing me with their lives.

Thanks to my brothers and sisters, who will recognise at least some of the material in *Artie*!

Josh and Jo Yeldham – fellow travellers, thanks for your creative generosity.

Most of all thanks to Silvia Colloca. *Tutto questo e ancora di più*.

ABOUT THE AUTHOR

RICHARD ROXBURGH is one of Australia's best-loved and most versatile actors. For his work in films like *Moulin Rouge!* and *Van Helsing*, to the lead role in TV's *Rake*, as well as his many highly acclaimed performances with the Sydney Theatre Company, Richard Roxburgh has become a household name.

Richard has been successful on the other side of the camera too. He directed the feature film *Romulus, My Father* and was co-creator of the award-winning television series *Rake*. Richard has always drawn and written stories to entertain himself, but *Artie and the Grime Wave* is his first book for children.